Georgette couldn't believe how nervous she was. She patted her forehead with her silk scarf. She would be glad when the wait was over. The anticipation was too much for her to bear. She had to compose herself before she saw Ray. Breathing slowly would help, she decided. It *had* to.

Just as she had begun her breathing exercise, she glanced up to see a tall figure standing several feet away, his back to her. "Oh my gosh," she heard herself utter. If he looked as good in front as from behind, she would scream.

She stood there for what seemed like an eternity until she got up enough courage to walk over to him and tap him on the back. Her heart was doing the flip-flop song as he turned slowly to greet her. He held a bouquet of white roses surrounded by baby's breath, which he promptly lavished upon her.

"Hello, gorgeous," he said with a smile as he bent down to kiss her cheek.

"Hi, Ray," she whispered. "The roses are beautiful. Thank you."

"Anything for my Nubian queen," he answered with a bow. "Anything at all."

MONIQUE GILMORE

No Ordinary Love

PINNACLE BOOKS
WINDSOR PUBLISHING CORP.

This book is dedicated to my loving parents,
Herman & Janeth Gilmore;
my supportive brother, "Joey" Gilmore; and
my dedicated sister, Renee Gilmore.
God bless you and thank you forever.

PINNACLE BOOKS are published by

Windsor Publishing Corp.
850 Third Avenue
New York, NY 10022

First Pinnacle Printing: November, 1994

Printed in the United States of America

One

Cruising to the Fresh Prince's remake of one of Kool and the Gang's songs, Georgette was preparing for a fabulous weekend. It was a hot and humid day and the brothers and sisters were out in droves. The smell of barbecue and a variety of summer fragrances swept the air. She had the volume on the Alpine stereo cranked up to five and the sunroof flipped open. Peeking in the rearview mirror out of habit, she glided on more sassy red lipstick to accentuate her full lips. Still gazing in the mirror, she focused on the small dab of color outlining her high cheekbones. The sun had certainly evened out her skin tone, which was now a smooth, rich nutmeg color. After wiping away any signs of smeared mascara, she slid on her gold-trimmed Ray Ban's to cut the glare of the intense sunset from her hazel eyes. She pushed the specs further down on the bridge of her nose to keep her long eyelashes from brushing up against the glass. Quickly assessing her place in traffic, she grabbed a brush out of her purse and ran it through her golden brown hair three times.

Rocking her head back and forth to the groove of the music, Georgette elicited many stares from the neighboring cars at the light. She needed to be in the right lane before the next intersection, so she glanced at the driver to her right and then at the one to her left, wanting to fake them both out before the light changed. She gunned the four-cylinder engine at the first flash of green. Adjusting the rearview mirror as she drove, she grinned a half-moon smile. She beat them!

The car screamed for mercy as she skidded into the Wash-n-Wax lot. She eased over to the entrance line while checking out the wash menu.

"How you doing today? You want the works?" asked the six-foot-one-inch figure cloaked in blue denim.

"What's the special today?" she asked.

"The usual. Ten bucks for a wash and hot wax. You should let me Armor All them tires. When's the last time you had them done?"

Was this mechanic trying to hustle her? Georgette wondered. She had the works done on the car just two weeks ago. She stepped out of the car and gave the attendant a level gaze. "How much more?" she asked.

"Only three dollars," he said, smiling as he stole a peek at her thighs. "Per tire."

"Per tire? More like twelve dollars then, huh?"

"Yeah, but you need all four of them done," he said, winking at her.

"That's fine, I just didn't want any surprises at the checkout counter, you know?"

What the heck, Georgette figured. Twelve dollars didn't make that much difference in her life. For some people, the amount could be a matter of life or death. She tried to help out where she could. She'd just given the kid at the corner a few streets back a dollar for wiping her windows even though she was on her way to the car wash. The kid was trying, she knew, working hard in the heat while other kids were at camp or grandma's house for the summer.

The attendant handed her the receipt and motioned her to go inside to pay the bill. She waited until they finished vacuuming the interior of the car, then placed a few dollars in the tip box. The men thanked her, and their appreciative stares lingered perhaps a bit too long before they went on to the next car.

Georgette glanced down at her attire. She attributed the many stares she was getting to the short white linen skirt and matching raw silk tee top she was wearing. She had left her jacket draped over the passenger seat to keep it from wrinkling after having taken it off after work. She was careful to cover up while at the newspaper office.

She grabbed a pine tree air freshener as she handed the clerk the twenty. It was hot in the waiting area, and she imagined with pleasure the cool bathwater that would engulf her body as soon as she got home.

"Thank you," she said with a smile, handing two more dollars to the brothers drying off her car before she got in, pumped the stereo volume back up, and carefully merged into traffic.

Pulling into the driveway of her apartment, she could see her neighbor sitting in front of his window. She loved the two-story brick house because it reminded her of her grandmother's.

"Need some help?" yelled Mr. Burke from his upstairs window.

"I've got it, thanks," replied Georgette. She was used to a solo mission when it came to lugging in packages. Today, however, she had more than the usual load. She was swamped with grocery bags, bags from the cleaners, bags from the video store, and a bag of fresh-cut flowers from the florist. She didn't mind making the three trips back and forth from her first-floor apartment to the silver Honda Accord. The neighborhood was safe, and she could leave the front door open until the job was done.

Mr. Burke, the superintendent of the building, gladly offered a helping hand whenever he saw her loaded down with stuff. He was an elderly man in his late sixties, but sported a look as young as forty. A widower for the past three years, he was finally plunging into the dating scene again. "Things sure have changed since my dating days. Some women will do just about anything to be with a man," he would frequently say to Georgette. Georgette would just shrug and vow she'd never be one of those women.

"Finally!" exclaimed Georgette, "the last of the bags." She locked the door behind her, grabbed the remote control to the stereo, and flicked on the CD player. The voice of Phil Perry filled the room as she unpacked the bags and shelved the grocery items. She put the fresh-cut flower arrangement she had bought in the Waterford vase and filled it with spring water. She was going to prepare a little snack for herself and relax before the start of her big evening. She planned to make her secret seafood dish for the special dinner tonight. But suddenly she realized how exhausted she was from running so many errands. She decided to have a glass of water and steal some shut-eye after unloading the last bag.

Nestling down into her soft, oversized African-patterned sofa, Georgette let the cool mountain spring water soothe her parched throat. She kicked off her lizard pumps, letting the size sevens glide through the plush hunter green carpet. Deciding to try to catch the weather report for the weekend, she stretched for the remote to the TV. "Aw, dang," she muttered. "I have to do something about all these remote controls." The JVC remote on the coffee table was for the VCR; she wanted the Sony remote for the TV. She glanced quickly around the earth-toned living room until she spotted it next to the tall CD rack. "One of these days I will have a universal remote," she said, frowning as she pressed the power button and selected channel four for the news.

At first, she didn't know what to make of the furious flames and pieces of debris scattered before her on the twenty-seven-inch screen. Then she noticed the caption that read "Live from Chicago." For a while she thought the station was experiencing technical difficulties. The sounds of the TV were fading in and out, as was the picture. Apparently the cameraman was having a hard time keeping his balance; the picture kept swaying in and out of focus. When the sound did fade in, the reporter's voice did not project over the loud noise, confusion, and sirens in the backdrop. Everything on the screen was absurdly bright, from the camera lights to the orange flames in the near distance. What was the reporter saying? *What's happening here?* she wondered agitatedly. Something is wrong with the TV, she thought, pressing the remote buttons frantically.

But once Georgette hit the carpet, she knew it wasn't the station that was experiencing the technical difficulty—it was her brain. Had she heard right? Flight 2830 from Chicago bound to Philadelphia had crashed upon takeoff?

"Oh my God!" she cried. "Flight from Chicago? Please no, no, no!" she screamed, clinching her elbows and rocking back and forth on her knees. "Please no, not flight twenty-eight thirty!"

She glared expressionless at the TV as the tears burned down her cheeks. Her stomach was a part of her throat now. Her heart, her breathing was constricted; her lungs felt like they were being compressed against her back. She waited for more information. "Come on" she pleaded, "please, please let there be no casualties."

The news hit her in the chest like a ton of bricks sailing off of the back of a speeding pickup truck. Her eyes rolled up into the back of her head as she fought to remember how to breathe. She was suffocating to death; she needed to inhale but her brain wouldn't remind her how. The shades of the room were fading as she fell face-forward onto the floor. Georgette knew her life was skidding to an end when she heard the reporter announce, "No survivors."

Two

Earlier that year.

The winter season in Philadelphia was Gerard's least favorite time of the year. He sprinted through the campus with his coat collar full-mast. The fierce wind seemed to be directly channeling the snow flurries into his face. He unavoidably inhaled a few flakes as he attempted to duck for cover. Gerard loved the East Coast but dreaded the awful winters. He felt the dampness penetrating his lambskin-lined leather coat. Stuffing his hands further into the pockets, he tucked his chin under the collar. Simply put, it was damn cold. The thermometer read fifteen degrees, but he knew with the windchill factor it was more like five below.

Once inside the student center at Temple University, he shook his head viciously and the liquified snow sprayed a few students passing by. People on the East Coast sure are brave, Gerard thought. Or crazy. He wondered what the students at Cal Berkeley or

Stanford University were doing while he removed the rubber covers from his shoes. There seemed to be no one left on earth who wore the ugly black galoshes but him. His fraternity brothers wouldn't be caught dead in them, he knew. Then again, they never looked as good as he did in the winter.

The girls were starting to cast their scent already. Fragrances of "Hey good-looking," "Wonder if he's single," and "I sure would like to . . ." were in the air. Gerard gave off an aura of his own that replied "Maybe I am, maybe I will, maybe I won't." It took him the entire walk across the center, coupled with a large cup of hot chocolate, to thaw out. Finally slipping out of his leather coat, he wrapped it around his arm. He had on a thick gray turtleneck under a burgundy button-down brushed wool sweater. His newly polished black shoes complemented the black snakeskin belt he wore. The women were impressed, he could gather, and wanted him to pursue. But Gerard had himself already been pursued and was, at least temporarily, snagged.

Reaching the small room in the back of the student center, he straightened his turtleneck and sweater. He couldn't have the pledgees thinking he was a sloppy big brother.

The music room was marked RESERVED. Adjacent to the student union, the room was convenient and private. The fraternity used it to meet with pledgees. The room's small picture window had been blacked out. A baby grand piano and two blackboards were the only furnishings. Pushing the door open, Gerard was immediately saluted.

"Greetings, Big Brother Suave," harmonized the Fearsome Four lampados, the pledgees, as Gerard entered the room.

"Get out of my face, you punks," snarled Gerard, turning instead to greet his fellow fraternity brothers with the traditional Omega Psi Phi handshake.

"What's up, shorty? What brings you out this evening?" Brother Slim questioned, decked out in purple and gold paraphernalia. "Where's your ball and chain? I mean wife?" he teased. Slim's name accurately described him—a six-feet-four-inch, 180-pound brother who favored a giraffe.

Gerard gave him the usual middle finger flip. Ever since he had hooked back up with Georgette, the frat brothers had a thing too many to say. "Yo, you know she ain't stepping out without me," Gerard said dismissively. "Besides, she is so preoccupied with this engagement thing that I could disappear for a week and she wouldn't even trip."

"Yeah, right!" chuckled Big Brother Chauncey, whose line name had been Horse when he pledged because of his massive physique and bald head. The name also reflected his tenacity—he worked harder than any of the other fraternity brothers at the Temple chapter.

"Please, that's why you're about to jump the broom to make sure she don't sweep your ass. Don't try that macho man act with us. We know Georgette gave you the piss or get off the pot S&D and you danced. All the way to Tiffany's, I might add, to purchase that four-thousand-dollar rock," teased Larry, who stood at five-eleven in his dark blue business suit and round wire-framed glasses. He was 220 pounds and his mocha face was perfectly round like a moon.

"Yeah, well, just because we're engaged doesn't mean it's a signed-and-sealed deal. In fact, when I pick her up from the airport later tonight we'll have to talk. I received word today that Rutgers Law School will be giving me a partial fellowship. It looks like we'll need to reevaluate our situation."

"Congratulations on the fellowship deal," Slim said, grasping Gerard's hand. "But I don't know how your old lady is going to feel about this so-called reevaluation."

"I'm not worried about her. Either she'll handle it or she won't. Anyway, when is this sorry line crossing over?"

Gerard studied the pledgees for a while, reflecting on their physical flaws, which were well summed up by their line names. Bubbles, the number one man on line, acquired the name because of his protruding eyes and wild dark curly hair. Pledgee number two, Mr. Ed, got stuck with his name because of his teeth and their uncanny resemblance to that of a certain TV horse. Pledgee number three, Hook, got his name because of the lump in the back of his head. The last pledgee, Sticks, was six-three and weighed in at a mere 165 pounds, soaking wet. All of the pledgees' heads had been shaved bald and they ranged in order of height from five-eight to six-three. They were dressed in army pants and shirts and steel-toed black army boots. Despite their flaws, these pledgees were a nice-looking bunch of brothers, Gerard thought. However, he was strictly forbidden to give the little line brothers any encouragement whatsoever. The purpose of this pledge process was to find out who had the strength to endure and whether or not they would gel together as a unit to survive. Humiliation was definitely one of the ways the big brothers would try to break them down. That was the history behind the line names, after all.

After examining the last pledgee, Gerard broke out in a wild, hysterical laugh and asked his other three fraternity brothers, "So, when are they scheduled to become men?"

"Yo, the way I see it, they ain't crossing over. Not today, not tomorrow, or next month for that matter," yelled Big Brother Larry while poking the number two line man, Mr. Ed, in the chest.

"I say they don't know what it is or what it takes to be Omega men," said Gerard derisively.

"Big Brother Suave, we are willing to dedicate our lives to learn what it takes to become men like you," bellowed line man number one.

"Did Big Brother Suave ask you to speak?" interrogated Slim.

"No sir! Big Brother Slim."

"Well then, shut the hell up! Matter of fact, everybody assume the position!" barked Larry, grabbing the wooden paddles.

"My fellow Omega brothers, I don't think these lampados have learned a damn thing!" smirked Gerard. "Hit the lights!"

Three

"Come on Georgette!" Melinda commanded, walking slightly ahead. The complimentary shuttle bus heading toward Vail Village ski area would be at the stop in two minutes. It was difficult enough trudging through all the snow lugging skis and boots, but the altitude made it even harder. Melinda certainly did not want to miss the shuttle because of Georgette's short legs. Missing the shuttle meant they would have to return to the condo in all the snow with all their stuff. Melinda seemed to always end up with midgets for friends, she thought, flagging the shuttle down.

The shuttle bus was bursting at the seams when the driver skidded to a halt. Placing the skis on the rack attached to the side of the bus, the women squeezed their way onto the vehicle. The driver, somewhat catatonic from all the loud laughter and conversation, didn't bother to clarify their destination. His guess was that Georgette and Melinda had traveled his route for the entire week and knew exactly where they wanted to go.

It had been a nonstop party in Vail since the National Brotherhood of Skiers arrival a week ago. Georgette and Melinda didn't miss a beat. They attended every event on the calendar and then some. Initially, they had set out to have a carefree week of downhill skiing. They factored in a few parties here and there with opportunities of developing new acquaintances. They never imagined in their wildest fantasies that they would have such an exciting, invigorating week. The infamous NBS pajama party was what committed them to returning next year for the mini-summit so that they could see all the handsome brothers. There was such a beautiful array of well-groomed, articulate, witty, respectful brothers sliding around the entire week. Some were married, some not. Some were looking, some not. There were no drivebys, no "crack" downs, no homicides, no gangbanging, no *Eyewitness, Hard Copy, Unsolved Mysteries, Untold Stories, 911 or Code 3.* Just thousands of African-American men and women sliding and gliding, slipping but not tripping. Yup, they vowed to come back every year if they could afford it, Georgette thought. Matter of fact, it was going to be mandatory. Save now, play later is what she and Melinda agreed to last night. Georgette, absorbing the panoramic views, was interrupted by her best friend's sentence.

"What you thinking about?"

"Ray," Georgette responded dreamily. *Who else?* She smiled quietly to herself, drifting back into her daze. As if Melinda didn't know. The girl was standing right next to her the night she laid eyes on the tall, debonair gentleman. It was their second night at the summit and the Chicago ski group was having a house party. Ray was in charge of collecting the cover charge at the door.

Replaying the meeting over and over in her head, Georgette still could not believe how his resonant voice had sent chills through her body when he'd greeted them. Just thinking about it now sent a shiver through her.

"Good evening, ladies," he had said smoothly, and Georgette had had to lift her head back a good bit to return the greeting. He was dressed in a soft yellow cashmere jacket overlaying a black turtleneck and a pair of black, white, and gray checkered slacks. He was over six feet tall and had a tight build under the loose clothing. It was his smooth, dark tone, coupled with his confident smile, that sent her heart skipping.

Melinda neglected to mention the cover charge before they left the condo so they hadn't bothered to bring any cash. Once the embarrassment of that wore off, Georgette attempted to explain the situation to Ray.

He smiled, slid into her personal space, swooped up her hands to his chest, and uttered, "Tell you what, if you promise to save me the pleasure of a dance later on, you, your girlfriend, and the next five people that walk in after you won't have to pay a penny."

From that moment forward, the evening played out like a scene from a romantic fairy tale. There was something genuine about his kindness and warm smile. She tried to escape the impact he had made on her by getting lost in the crowd of people. But his cologne, which lingered on her hands, was a constant reminder. When Ray finally did trudge through the crowd to rescue her from some drunk man's rap, she was so elated she nearly jumped onto his chest.

He softly seized her hand and led her through the multitude of folks to the kitchen, where he offered her some fresh pineapple juice and buffalo wings. After he prepared their plates, he whisked her off to the solarium, where the only illumination in the room came from the brightness of the full moon and the many scattered stars. She found herself being sucked into his deep, sincere, deliberate voice; his lasting, spicy aroma; his soft embrace of her hands; and his intense gaze. Even though the room was dark, she could still catch the twinkle in his eye once in a while. And feel the tingle in her hands every so often. His gracefulness and unre-

lenting attention to her needs was over-
whelming. When the evening was over, she
realized she hadn't fulfilled her promise of
a dance and that he hadn't pressured her
either. He got her and Melinda's jackets,
helped them put them on, and then walked
them to their car.

Helping her into the car, he leaned in and
said, "I didn't forget about the dance. We'll
have plenty of opportunities this week for
that. But I would like to meet you for lunch
at noon tomorrow at the lodge. You don't
have to answer now. If I don't see you tomorrow, I'll know your answer. Good night, Georgette, and thanks for a memorable night."

Boom! Just like that, he had swept her off
her feet, and continued to do so in the days
that followed.

She shook her head slightly, gave a grin,
and unconsciously sighed, "Ray."

"Ray, Ray, Ray, that's all I've heard this
week," teased Melinda. "What about your
man—rather, your fiancé. Georgette? Did you
forget about Gerard already?"

"No, I haven't forgotten about him. But I
could be doing much worse than sharing
some simple conversation with a brother
while sliding down the slopes. I wouldn't
cheat on Gerard."

"Yeah, well, I'm sure Gerard's fraternity
brothers won't waste any time giving him the
scoop about your newfound private ski in-

structor when they get back home." Both
girls laughed, imagining what the frat brothers would say to Gerard: "Yo, man, we saw
your girl profiling with some lowlife at the
ski summit."

"Forget them," said Georgette. "They
didn't bother running to tell me that Gerard
was messing around with one of our sorority
sisters, so later for them. After all, there is
no telling what Gerard and his noncommit-
ting frat brothers get into when I'm not
around. This is the National Brotherhood of
Skiers ski summit and everyone knows that
it's just one big networking party." Georgette
smiled. "Besides," she continued, "Gerard
had an opportunity to attend the summit
with me, but as usual he had some lame excuse."

"Georgette, I don't know how or why you
keep hanging on. But if the brother makes
you happy, so be it."

Georgette sighed and looked Melinda directly in her eyes. "I know how you feel about
Gerard, Melinda, but he's changing his
ways."

"Oh yeah? How's that? So he drops a few
bills on you here and there. The bottom line
is, he is always *there* and never *here*. You know,
by your side?"

"Yeah, I know, but . . . Never mind,"
smirked Georgette. "Let's hit the powder.

I'm supposed to meet Ray at the lodge for happy hour before we head to the airport."

"This is the AT&T operator, may I help you?"

"Yes, I would like to make a call and charge it to my calling card."

"Thank you, sir. Have a good day," echoed the operator. Ray fumbled to place his card in his wallet as the call was connected.

"Yeah!" snapped the voice on the other end after one ring.

"Hey Joe, what's up? This is Ray."

"Hey man, I apologize for the greeting. I've been trying to lay this last track, but the phone hasn't stopped ringing. How's the trip?"

"Great! Joe, I think I'm in love."

"Get the heck out of here. With who?"

"A fine honeysuckle named Georgette," Ray intoned.

"Georgette, huh? Well, did you get some shots on the camcorder of this princess? Ray? Ray! Did you hear me?"

"Sorry about that, Joe," he paused while switching the phone to his left ear so that he could turn to face the four women approaching him in their bright-colored ski outfits. He tucked the phone under his chin and rested it on his left shoulder in order to tuck both his hands into his ski pants. "I'm temporarily mesmerized by this mosaic entourage of sisters, café au lait to espresso, strolling past me. There are so many fine women up here, my man. You should be here."

"Well, bring one of them back to Chicago for me," laughed Joe. "What time you getting in?"

"Around eleven P.M., from Denver."

"So, what else has been going on in Vail other than the women? Did you win any races?"

"What do you mean, what else is there besides these lovely ladies? Check it out, I'll tell you all about it when I get home. Here comes Ms. Georgette now."

"Okay, I'll see you later, man."

"See you," Ray said, hanging up the phone and swinging around to greet Georgette.

"Hey, beautiful, fancy seeing you here. Are you headed up to the slopes?"

"Only if you are," flirted Georgette. "You coming, Melinda?"

"Naw, you guys go ahead," Melinda answered, patting Georgette on the shoulder. "I see some people over there I want to talk to. I'll catch up with you at happy hour. Don't forget the airport shuttle will be here to pick us up in a few hours."

"Don't worry, Melinda, I'll have her back in time," smiled Ray.

"You'd better. See you guys later."

Ray reached out and grasped Georgette by the hand. Georgette fell right in sync, leaning into his chest. She could feel the magnetic attraction immediately, but was no longer alarmed by it. Perhaps that was because she had given up the battle to fight it earlier on in the week. How could she resist a brother that exuded such confidence, especially when that brother had Ray's rich, dark complexion, broad chest, tight buttocks, and perfect set of teeth to go along with his contagious smile? What would be the point? Why even bother? He managed to keep that alluring look even after a hard day of skiing. Georgette wondered how he was able to keep his strong, spicy scent with him no matter the time of day. Simply put, this brother was fine, she acknowledged silently, as he led the way to the lift, his hand in hers.

Finishing his last set of sit-ups, Gerard stretched for the phone. He listened briefly to the chattering voice on the other end before interrupting. "I don't think that would be a good idea, Cheryl. I have to pick Georgette up in a few hours. Look baby, you know I'm engaged now, so what's up with you? Okay, then, but I really think it would be to your detriment if we get together tonight. All right, just remember what I told you. See you in a while."

Gerard hung the phone up upside down, a habit he had developed while pledging. It was a way for him to detect if someone had used his phone without his permission. It was human nature for people to hang the phone up correctly. Human nature for people to do correct things, period. So now why was he about to do the morally incorrect thing? He had patched things up with Georgette not even two months ago and now he was at it again.

Flipping through the oak hangers in his closet, looking for just the right apparel, he wondered: Would or could he ever commit to Georgette, or anyone else for that matter? Could he remain faithful? Gerard imagined what Georgette would do if she found out he was cheating on her. If she found out that once again his love for her was not as strong as his love for himself and his desires.

Tucking his charcoal turtleneck under a black cashmere sweater, he pondered the question of why Georgette was still dealing with him anyway? Sade's soothing notes were oozing out of the Bose 901s. "Oh well," he dismissed aloud. "She knows how I am. She's known me for five years. If she's willing to deal, then I'm not going to worry about it." He splashed on some *Eternity*, groomed his mustache, and brushed his teeth.

The thought occurred to him that maybe what he was doing was simply buying time.

Time to grow to the point where he wouldn't need to commit to anyone but himself.

"Keys, keys," he whispered while searching the coffee table. "I'll take the BMW tonight. That always impresses Cheryl." He located the key chain with the initials BMW, lifted the stereo remote, and disengaged the system. He would leave the halogen lamp dimmed so that the heated aroma of the light bulb ring would greet him upon his return.

Glancing for one last time in the large mirror secured between the mahogany wall unit, he brushed his hands across his hair and uttered, "God, you're one good-looking brother!" Now he was ready to step out, and into Cheryl's boudoir.

Four

The ride on the chairlift up the mountain was usually brisk, but today Georgette found the journey exceptionally warm. She huddled against Ray, absorbing his heat. Here in the powdered Rocky Mountains, Georgette thought about how much she enjoyed skiing and how she wished Gerard was into it as much as she. But she was riding on the chairlift with a man other than her fiancé, enjoying his company as much as she enjoyed the view.

"The mountains are so beautiful," Georgette said.

"Yes, they sure are," replied Ray, placing his arm around Georgette's shoulder and pulling her closer.

Georgette noticed the steam rolling from his nostrils as he breathed. She wanted to know if his kisses were as gentle as he was.

Ray wondered about the ring on Georgette's left ring finger. What exactly was its significance? He could not imagine why she had been hanging out so much with him all week. Not that it really mattered. Even though he wanted to respect her beau, whoever and wherever he might be, this time he took the attitude "available until married."

"Well, do you want to ski the back China bowls or take the whimpy route?" Georgette asked.

Ray grinned and replied, "I just love a sister who is aggressive on the slopes. Let's see what you're made of and ski the back bowls."

"And I love a brother who can issue a challenge. Let's roll! And Ray, do try and keep up."

Before she had a chance to lift off, Ray lifted his goggles and reeled Georgette to his chest. He could feel how soft her breasts were even through all the ski gear. He raised her goggles over her headband, gazed into her hazel eyes, and whispered, "I wish we had another week here." Tipping her head back ever so slightly, he pressed his lips against hers. He kissed her slowly three times before reluctantly pulling away. The kiss was the beginning of Ray's hopes and dreams to interpret Georgette's feelings.

Melinda heard her name called from somewhere across the dance floor. Something about the voice made her pulse quicken. When she turned, she saw why.

"Don, is that you? Oh my God, how you

doing?" she said, crossing over to the man, then awkwardly wrapped her arms around his neck before kissing him softly on the cheek. Out of all the thousands of people at the summit, she never imagined that she would bump into her old love. They had dated when she was attending college and while he worked at the university as a technician. They broke up about three years ago and hadn't seen or talked to each other since.

"You look beautiful, Melinda. What did you say? Listen, the music is so loud I can barely hear you. Do you want to dance?"

"Sure," yelled Melinda over Teddy Riley & Wrecks & Effects' classic shaker song.

"How you enjoying the summit?" Don asked.

"It's been a lot of fun. I can't believe how many people are here."

"Seven thousand is the last report I heard. Did you go to any of the NBS parties?"

"Of course! The infamous pajama party and the African attire affair."

"Who are you here with?"

"Georgette. What about you?"

"A few buddies who belong to the Philadelphia ski group. We all needed a vacation. So, what you been up to, Melinda?"

"Just working and raising my little girl."

Don's mouth dropped open and he was silent for a moment before he spoke.

"You have a baby?"

Melinda nodded. "Elisha. She's a year old. I've got a picture of her at the table. Do you want to see it?"

Naughty By Nature's national anthem was now thumping the dance floor. Melinda gestured to Don that she wanted to head back to the table. He nodded in agreement and they waded through the dance crowd. Don was feeling a little awkward. It was hard to think of Melinda with a child. He tried to get his feelings in check before he reached the table. He was feeling disappointed and hurt. Hurt that she had had a child by someone else; hurt that he hadn't talked to her in almost three years; hurt because deep down he realized he still loved her.

"Want something to drink?" Melinda asked.

"No thanks," he said.

Melinda fumbled through her purse until she found her wallet. She reached behind the plastic picture holder and pulled out the picture of Elisha. "Here's my precious angel," she said, handing the picture to Don.

"She's gorgeous! She looks just like her mommy," he complimented, handing the picture back. Melinda sensed his discomfort; he had barely glanced at the picture. Melinda knew how uncomfortable he must feel. After all, she had been the one to end the relationship three years ago when it was apparent that Don wasn't the man of her dreams. She loved Don, but at that time she was looking for Mr. Right. Even though she knew that Don was a wonderful man, he had not seemed ambitious enough for her at the time. She wanted to marry a professional, a doctor, lawyer, someone with status, "someone with large bills," she would often say to her girlfriends. Yet Don had been good to her. In fact, he was better to her than any other man she had ever been with, including Elisha's daddy.

She had met Elisha's father, Greg, while he was completing his final year of residency as a neurologist. Melinda was graduating from college. He had everything she thought she wanted: status, prestige, money, a home, a Mercedes 190. Later she would learn that his only goal was to prove a point. That he could win her love for him over her love for Don. And at the time he had all the right tools, so it seemed, to win. He swept her off her feet with expensive gifts and then slapped a two-carat diamond on her finger in the Virgin Islands at a small chapel on the beach.

At the time, she had an incurable case of Buppie-itis and Don was not the cure. He was just a hardworking blue-collar mechanical technician for Penn State's psychology department. Melinda thought that it was a fairly good-paying job, earning about $2,900 per month, but that it wasn't the image she wanted the man in her life to project.

But now she saw that towering over her was

the man she should have married. The man that had given her unconditional love. The man who, when it came right down to it, was the best lover she had ever had. A man, she realized, she still loved.

"So, what about you, Don? Have you settled down? You have any children yet?"

"Not yet. Maybe one day." Don could now sense Melinda's own discomfort. He wondered if she still had feelings for him, and if so, then why hadn't he heard from her in all this time. She sure looked good, he thought. She still had that kiddish smile and that light voice. A little voice in such a strong five-foot-nine physique packed with curves. Her hair was still coal-black and full of body and shine; her skin, still dark and smooth. Don felt a stirring in his heart. The woman still excited him mentally, spiritually, and physically.

"Are you married?" he asked.

"Not anymore. What about you?"

"Still waiting for you," he said with a smirk.

Melinda blushed with pleasure. She'd have to invite this man up to New York soon. The way she figured, the drive from Philadelphia was only a few hours.

"You still living in Philly, Don?"

"Yup. You still in NYC?"

"Of course."

Don impulsively reached for Melinda and

wrapped his arms around her. Melinda held on tight. It had been a few full moons since she'd last hugged a man so tightly. When she buried her head into his chest, it felt like she had never left. God, how she missed this man. She could feel the tears welling up in her eyes as a sense of guilt washed through her. She knew she had hurt Don deeply. And that she had taken the coward's way out, thinking she could never face him again. That was the reason for the distance, the lost communication between them. A teardrop escaped from her bottom lid as she pressed him closer. An old tune by Johnny Gill was humming in the background.

"It's all right," Don whispered, kissing her forehead.

"I'm so sorry, Don," mumbled Melinda.

"I know, I know, baby," he said softly. "Melinda, I haven't stopped loving you."

"Oh, Don," she said in a quivery voice.

"Melinda," yelled Georgette.

Melinda jolted from Don's embrace, quickly wiping her eyes. She gestured to Georgette to wait a minute as she gathered her things from the table. Picking up a pen, she jotted her phone number and address on the back of a flyer. Turning, she gave Don the piece of paper, "Will you call me?"

"Of course I will," he promised, placing a small kiss on her lips. He jotted something down on a piece of paper. "Here's my new

number. Call me when you get in tonight.
I'll be up late. You can call me collect if you
want to—we need to talk, okay?"

"I will," promised Melinda. "And Don,
I'm really glad to see you. Talk to you soon,"
she said, placing a kiss on his cheek as she
rushed to join Georgette.

"Girl, was that Don I just saw you kissing?"
Georgette exclaimed.

"Yes," Melinda said breathlessly. "Girl, I'm
not going to lie, I still love that man."

"Well, I do say, girlfriend, I always knew
you two would connect again. Do you think
he'll give you another chance?"

"I don't know, Georgette. I can't think, my
head is swimming. What's happening with
you and Ray?"

"I'm not sure, but I can tell you that I've
thought about him all seven days this week."

"No kidding," teased Melinda.

"What I do know is, he has the softest lips
I've ever felt."

"What's this? Oh, so you did a little more
than just sliding down the slopes with Ray,
huh? Well, it's obvious the man's hot for
you."

"Well, now I've got to go home and face
Gerard. The sad thing is, I really wish we
had a few more nights here. I'm not ready
to return to Philly. I don't know, Melinda.
Something's up with me. It sure feels good
though."

"I think that's great, Georgette. You've been through so much this past year, you're about due for some true happiness." She thought about Gerard and his promiscuity, the breakups and reconciliations. Melinda had come to define happiness for Georgette as life without Gerard.

Five

"Look, Cheryl, I told you before I got over here that I couldn't stay. Georgette will be in soon and I've gotta pick her up."

"I know Gerard, jeez!" snapped Cheryl. "But we still have a few hours, so let's get something to eat. All this extracurricular activity has worked up my appetite."

"I'm not really hungry. Don't you have something in the kitchen you can fix?" Gerard could see that she was getting a little annoyed with his attitude, but he didn't care. He was just hanging out, no pressures, no expectations, no formal commitment. Besides, Cheryl knew the deal about him and Georgette. He had planned to take her to dinner, but decided not to risk bumping into any of her sorority sisters. The situation was already too tight, with Cheryl and Georgette belonging to the same sorority. He didn't want to make it any more snug by displaying his dishonesty openly.

"Gerard, the least we could do is run and

grab a quick bite somewhere. I'm starving and I don't feel like cooking."

"Try fasting then! Cheryl, I don't feel like moving okay? Not until it's time for me to go. Unless you are ready for me to leave now," he threatened.

"Well, could you at least spring for some Chinese if I order in?"

"Whatever, Cheryl. Wake me up in an hour so I can shower, all right?"

"Don't you want to be awake when the food gets here?"

"No. I told you, I'm not hungry. Here's a ten spot. That should cover it."

The nerve of this asshole, Cheryl thought. *Coming over here to lay up for a minute or two and can't even take me out to get a bite to eat. What's a lousy ten bucks supposed to buy?* She couldn't believe how damn cheap he was. He's got plenty of money, she thought. He's driving around in a BMW and a Jeep Grand Cherokee and sporting the latest Hugo Boss and Armani suits while telling time on a Movado or a Cartier. In addition to the fact that he'd been clocking almost three times her salary since he finished his MBA. Now he can't even spring for a flimsy dinner? She knew if Georgette were to ask him, he wouldn't hesitate. "That little heifer don't even have a clue about her so-called man," she huffed under her breath. *But that's okay,* she thought. *He's here with me now, so it doesn't really matter. If that prima donna wench only knew . . .*

Cheryl glanced over to the sofa where Gerard was laying. *He sure is one fine brother,* she thought. Maybe it's that body of his that keeps her from telling him to go to hell. Or it could be those dimples or that soft copper-colored skin. Maybe it's all that hair on his chest and legs, or that perfectly rounded butt. Perhaps it's all the fine clothing, the MBA status, the cars, that hinder her thoughts of escape. Whatever it is, she would endure, tolerate the situation just long enough in the hopes that she could finally seize Gerard, no matter what it would take.

Six

"Okay girlfriend, this is where we say goodbye for now," Georgette said, hugging Melinda.

"I'll probably drive down to Philly in a few weeks. Who knows, maybe it will be sooner than I think," Melinda grinned.

"All right then, call me tomorrow and let me know how things turn out after you talk to Don tonight. I'm supposed to go with Gerard to a Super Bowl party, but I'm sure it won't be until later on in the evening."

"Don't keep your legs elevated too long tonight," laughed Melinda.

"Why certainly, sister Melinda, we wouldn't want any of your good habits to rub off on me," Georgette yelled as she ran to catch her flight.

Settling down in her seat, Georgette gazed out the window. Two thoughts occupied her mind as the plane leveled off: One, how she despised the four-hour flight east, and two, why her baby brother Kyle felt obliged to remind her prior to her trip that not all black men who have degrees are good and not all good black men have degrees. She was well aware of this fact. Although Dorian, her older sister, would never consider dating a man, much less marrying one, without a college degree, Georgette never could understand what all the fuss was over a little piece of paper. After all, had it not been for their degree-less dad, Herbert Willis, Georgette, Kyle, Dorian and their mother, Jackie, would have all been homeless. Her mom was a homemaker and her father worked as a meter reader for the local gas and electric company for forty years. During those years, he effectively managed to raise three children, support her through college, and put Dorian through medical school.

But then, why hadn't she herself considered dating a man without a B.S. or B.A degree before? What could be so awful about linking up with a nondegreed, yet ambitious brother?

Her father, a retired technician of sorts, and her brother, an aircraft mechanic, were both nondegreed, hardworking, respectable, responsible, loving men.

How was it that she spun such a deadly web around Gerard? Yeah, so Gerard was what sisters referred to as a "Tenderoni": a well-built, handsome brother with strong shoulders, buffed hairy chest, and the firmest thighs you'd ever want to see. But he was a confirmed gonnabe, wannabe and always-would-be bachelor. *Commitment* was not in Gerard's vocabulary. He was the personification of bachelorhood. A graduate of Howard University and the one and only "Lone Dog" of Omega Psi Phi, the brothers referred to him as Suave Buck. Debonair at five-eleven, he had the gift of gab followed by a dedicated fan club. Why Gerard chose her among the flock she could never figure.

They had been dating for four years when, suddenly, one weekend Gerard needed to take a "piece of mind" solo trip to D.C., allegedly to visit some fraternity brothers. A piece of mind trip? she remembered clarifying with Gerard. Okay, she bought that until she saw him at the Black Expo in New York hugged up with Cheryl.

Oh, how she hated that trollop. They were rivals all through high school, and all through college. The competition was fierce between them from the onset. It all started during their high school years, when Cheryl decided to run for school president just because she wanted to prove to everyone she could beat Georgette. Then when Cheryl got wind that Georgette was solicited to run for prom queen, all hell broke loose. Cheryl tried her best to sabotage the campaign but to no satisfaction. Georgette had beat her opponent once again and was named prom queen and "most likely to succeed." From that point on,

Cheryl knew the only way she could get her goat was by attempting to seduce every boyfriend or male friend she came into contact with. For a while, Georgette believed that Cheryl was obsessed with getting the best of her. Why else would she attend the same college, take up the same major, pledge the same sorority, and try to steal Gerard from her?

She confronted them both that day at the Expo, trying her best to save her image. Did he even know how embarrassed she was to see him with another woman, who happened to be her soror, as well as her one and only enemy? She should have left him for good right then and there, but she just told him he wasn't worth the energy or effort and walked away.

This is probably the reason, Georgette knew, why he felt it necessary to purchase an engagement ring for her the following month. He was attempting to get out of the doghouse or, better yet, avoid the eternal kennel of damnation. Deep down she knew chances were that he wasn't at all genuine. But seeing all those bridal magazines while standing in line at the grocery store had zapped some of her brain cells. She had actually convinced herself that becoming Gerard's bride was going to be exciting. All along, she detected, just as her relatives and friends discerned, and just as Gerard knew, that he was buying and stealing time chewing up her life. She was permitting Gerard Jenkins, the grinder, to chew and spit, gnaw and spatter her life away.

But along comes Ray Fuschée to the rescue . . . The flight attendant broke off her thoughts with the words, "Chicken or fish, ma'am?"

"Fish," said Georgette distractedly as she returned to her daydream. Ray's a dazzling smooth chocolate man with a gorgeous body, any woman could see that. She loved the way his long eyelashes blinked with his every word. It was like he was talking with his eyes instead of his mouth. Not to mention that thundering baritone voice which resonated to her very core. She was a sucker for stimulating conversation.

A firefighter recently made lieutenant, Ray had two other seeming strikes against him: an ex-wife and a three-year-old boy. Putting that all aside, there seemed to be something unusual about Ray and the mesmerizing effect he had on her. Some sisters would sell their souls in order to secure what Ray believed in. He cherished marriage, companionship, loyalty, children, the whole Cinderella story. Even after experiencing the grueling effects of a divorce, Ray seemed not to display any bitterness.

Georgette dared to daydream one last time before dozing off into a slumber. She had to be very cautious with Fire Lieutenant Ray.

Simply put, he possessed the tools and experience that could penetrate the emotional wall surrounding the tenuously wrought castle where she resided with Gerard.

"Yo, Joe! Over here," yelled Ray.

"Man, I hate O'Hare," grumbled Joe. "This airport is too damn big! How was your flight?"

"I don't know. I slept the entire way."

"So give me the scoop on this new darling you met on the slopes," he said as he helped Ray with the luggage.

"Yeah, buddy, Ms. Georgette has definitely touched my soul. She's beautiful, bright, and she can ski her butt off! She is all of that man, I'm telling you," beamed Ray, placing his skis in the back of his Explorer.

"What does this nose opener do?" snickered Joe.

"She's an editor for the local newspaper in Philly."

"Philly? So she's one of them fly East Coast girls."

"Yeah, you could say that. You know what this means, right?" Ray asked.

"No, but I know you're about to tell me," teased Joe.

"It means I'll have to give ole Cousin Lynn a call and make plans to visit Philly."

"Damn, man, besides them happy trails,

what else did you guys do?" he asked with a wink.

"Ah, come on, Joe, can't a brother fall a little without it always being a sex thing?"

"You mean to tell me you've dived off before you even had a chance to curl up them toes?"

"Later for you, Joe! I'm going to call Lynn this week and see what her schedule looks like and make some plans to accumulate some more frequent flyer miles."

It had been awhile since Ray had spoken to his cousin Lynn. To be honest, it was at least six or seven months. It wasn't a big deal, Ray thought. They were like Frick and Frack. It never bothered Lynn or Ray if some time elapsed between their communication. They'd been close since the first grade. After his aunt Claudine relocated from Chicago to Philly, Lynn and Ray managed to remain tight. He would give her a call later this week after he spoke with Georgette. First he needed to find out if the feeling was mutual about his potential visit. Yeah, that's what he would do. Call Georgette and find out how she felt not only about his visit but about her current life. More specifically, how she felt about that brother who purchased that blinding rock on her finger. He wouldn't ask too many personal questions initially, just enough for her to provide him with concrete information.

"Hey, pull over to that pizza stand for a second, I'm starving," demanded Ray.

"Pizza, at this time of night? Brother, you better hurry up and get you a wife!" teased Joe.

"What, your first sister-in-law wasn't enough for you?" smiled Ray.

How could his little brother forget the hell that his ex-wife had put him through, he thought silently. Both his mother and sister hadn't forgotten the grief Rachel caused him over the divorce. His mom, a psychotherapist for the past fifteen years, would frequently remind him that he should be fighting for control over his own life and not someone else's. Oftentimes his sister Theresa, who had followed his mother's footsteps and become a therapist, would try to get him to "get in touch" with his true feelings about the breakup so that he wouldn't tote his baggage with him to some other woman's life. But all he wanted to do was bury that part of his story forever and move forward.

"Oh, before I forget. Rachel called a few days ago. Anthony wanted to speak to you. She said she'd give you a call when you got back."

"Yeah, right," mumbled Ray. How he fought on a daily basis not to blast his ex-wife. The mere mention of her name used to send him up in smoke. How could a married woman allow her love and her body to be invaded by another man? What the hell, he dismissed. Thank God there was Anthony. Ray had really wanted Rachel to name their baby after him, but they had argued the night she went into labor. He was fighting a three-alarm fire and had missed Anthony's delivery. Rachel, who was so angry at him for missing the birth, out of spite named the child Anthony.

Whatever Anthony might have been named, Ray was happy that he had a son. The one thing Ray knew he could count on was Anthony's bright smile and unconditional love. He couldn't wait until his fourth birthday so that he could teach him how to ski. He loved his son very much and wondered what would happen if he ever lost him, especially to another man. He couldn't imagine Anthony calling someone else "daddy." It would just kill him. But Rachel was trying hard to make such a nightmare come to life. Her new man, Douglas, wanted Anthony to address him as his father. Shortly after the divorce had been finalized, Ray went to Rachel's house to pick Anthony up for the weekend. When he heard Anthony refer to Douglas as Daddy upon their departure, he snatched Doug by the collar, nearly snapping his neck. He told Doug that Anthony already had a father and warned that he better never forget it.

Rachel got a kick out of it, as usual. It was then that he finally realized how Rachel had manipulated him during their entire relationship, from start to finish. She had been the spoiled, favored, youngest child who whined and fretted about any and everything she wanted. Besides her father and himself, Ray wondered how any man could stand her self-centered ways. "My daddy" this, "my daddy" that, it went on nonstop, he remembered. Her daddy had not been that fond of her marrying an average brother. He wanted his little girl to be a kept woman, never having to lift a finger if she didn't want to. This, too, was hard for Ray to deal with. How do brothers do it? he wondered. Putting up with unnecessary crap from the in-laws, coupled with the fact that your wife is undermining your marriage. Well, Rachel's daddy got his wish. Apparently, his little girl finally snagged the big one, Dr. Douglas Rich. *Good luck, Doug,* Ray thought with a smirk, *because you will definitely never have any money.*

Seven

"He's late!" Georgette murmured, snatching her bags off the luggage carousel. "I told him twelve forty-five A.M., baggage area." *It's now straight up one-ten and he is nowhere to be found,* she thought, strolling over to the oversized doors to pick up her skis. Gerard purchased her some new Rossignol 185s and the Nordica boots before her trip. It was another guilt purchase in an attempt by him to restore the peace. *So where the heck is he?* She grabbed a dollar from her wallet and rented a luggage cart. She hoped he was outside. He knew how much stuff she had. Why wasn't he inside to help her?

Once outside, Georgette glanced around at the parked cars. She finally noticed the smoky gray BMW double-parked a few feet away. Why in the world would Gerard pick her up in the beemer? He knew she had her ski gear. When he had tried to pack the equipment in the car after they purchased it, the gear wouldn't fit without infringing on the driver and passenger space. *So what's he*

*been doing that he had to parade and profile in
the beemer?* She could feel a slight increase in
her blood pressure as she tapped on the window. Gerard popped out like a jack-in-the-box. "Hey, babe," he said, winding around
to the back of the car by her side.

"Hey," Georgette said as happily as she
could.

"How was your trip?" he asked, placing the
bags in the car. He was looking somewhat
puzzled, trying to figure out what to do with
the skis.

"Where's the Jeep?"

"Home. I forgot you had these damn skis."
He crossed the skis between the backseat and
the front seat. "This should do it."

He wondered if Georgette sensed that he
had been up to something. Then it dawned
on him. "Where's my kiss?"

Georgette planted a faint kiss on his lips.
She sensed immediately that he had been up
to no good. He only drove the BMW when
he was trying to impress someone. He always
dressed well, but Georgette decided he
looked much too refreshed for such a late
hour. Georgette figured that if Gerard had
come from home, he would have thrown on
some Nikes and sweats. If he had been out
with the bros he would be that much worse
for wear. So just exactly what had he been
up to? She sucked her teeth as she attempted
to stop the negative self-talk. How could she

even think about marrying this brother if she didn't trust him?

"So, what did you do tonight?" The words were out of her mouth before she could stop herself.

"Not too much. We have a line going over soon, so I stopped by to pay my respects."

"You look awfully nice and you're driving the beemer. I just figured you had some special event or something."

"Georgette," Gerard said calmly. "Please don't start. It's late and I'm tired."

"You don't look so tired to me. But then again, that's just my perception."

Oh God, Gerard thought. He couldn't believe that she knew him so well. What a sleuth she was. He would have to be more careful. Then Gerard's thoughts took a different turn. He began wondering why Georgette hadn't greeted him with one of her powerhouse kisses when he got out of the car. It seemed strange to Gerard that Georgette wasn't pressed for a hug or a kiss. She'd been gone for over a week. *So what gives with her?* "Do you want to go home or come over to my place?" Gerard posed.

"I'm feeling a little tired, Gerard. I guess I'll go home." *Now for sure something's up,* Gerard thought. How in the world can you be gone from your flame all week and not want to ignite the fire upon your return? He replayed the question over and over in his head. The dead calm in the car was stiller than he could stand. Maybe there was lipstick on his collar or a woman's scent lingering on his shirt. Or maybe she had met someone at the summit. His frat brothers had tried to warn him that he should accompany Georgette for insurance purposes. Gerard felt jealousy swelling in his chest contributing to the change in his breathing. He didn't know what he would do if he ever found out she was screwing around on him, especially with that four-thousand-dollar marquise on her finger.

The beemer was still gliding into park when Georgette flung open the car door and jumped out.

"Could you at least wait until I stop the car?" he asked. Georgette said nothing as she continued walking toward the trunk. They were at her front door before she knew it. She fumbled for her keys, a rather annoying habit she had, Gerard thought. He never could figure out why she didn't have her keys ready before she reached the door.

Once inside, Gerard noticed how nicely plump she looked from behind. He could feel his pants growing tight as he planted a kiss on the back of her neck.

Georgette felt more obligated than genuinely interested when she turned around to respond. He grabbed her by her waist and drew her near. She didn't try to fight it.

Damn, the man could get to her! She realized how much he must have missed her as they touched down onto her queen-sized antique sleigh bed.

"I missed you," Gerard whispered.

"I've missed you, too," she said, wondering if her words could convince them both.

Eight

"Interception!" screamed Joe as he did his rendition of the Cowboys' celebration dance. "It's all over, brother," he continued.

But Ray didn't respond. He was engrossed in his thoughts of Georgette. He'd rather be in the game between Georgette and her fiancé instead of cheering for a dysfunctional AFC team. How the AFC teams remained a part of the National Football League after years of "back to back" Super Bowl defeats amazed him.

But oh, how he wanted to have the strength and persistence of the NFC teams and win Georgette's love. Maybe he was jumping the gun a little. Or maybe it was his inner spirit that was telling him she was an angel sent from above.

He imagined what his buddies would say. What his family would say. The comments, clear and sharp like a needle piercing the skin. "Have you lost your mind? You've only known her for a week and now you're ready to jump the broom?" his mother and sister would say. His buddies would accuse him of being whipped, but Ray didn't care.

He sprang up from the leather recliner to retrieve more refreshments. He would have to ride this wave out with Georgette and find out if he had the strength to endure. Sensing Georgette's attraction, he knew it was deeper than the skin thing. It was more like a direct spiritual hookup.

"You want another brewski, man?" Ray asked his cousin Ali.

"Naw, I'm cool, thanks."

"Since it's halftime, let's check out that videotape from the ski summit," Joe said, positioning the tape into the VCR. A few seconds into the video, there were a group of seventy people or so doing the electric slide in the ski lodge. Everyone was dressed in assorted ski gear and jamming to the music. The lodge was a huge room filled with people dancing, talking, walking, or just admiring the view. It wasn't long into the tape before Ray snatched the VCR remote from the sofa arm and hit the pause button.

"There she is right there," he said.

The silence in the room was deafening.

"She's gorgeous!" exhaled his buddies in unison.

"We will have to make that trip next year for sure," roared Miguel.

"So, what's the four-eleven on Ms. Georgette, Ray?" asked Ali.

"I don't know it all yet but I can tell you that she seemed as intrigued as me."

"What exactly does that mean? Did you do some friendly bonding or not?" teased Keith.

"Is that all you horny, early ejaculating brothers think about?" Ray asked.

"Oh, like you don't?" laughed Joe

"No, not all the time," Ray defended.

"That's bullshit!" they all yelled, turning the TV back to the game.

"All BS aside, man, I wish the best for you and Ms. Texas, I mean Georgia," snickered Ali.

"Her name is Georgette, you lowlife son of a—"

"Alabama, Texas, Georgia, whatever. Just good luck," grinned Ali.

Yeah, thought Ray, closing the bedroom door behind him. He would need more like a miracle to help him with this one. Lifting the receiver from its cradle, he began dialing the eleven digits. He needed to talk with Georgette now and see her soon. It was too late to turn back. Ray was falling hard.

Nine

"Mommy," Elisha's little hands smoothed over Melinda's face.

"Hey, precious," mumbled Melinda, still suffering from jet lag.

"Doggie? Mommy, doggie?" Elisha pleaded in her little voice.

"No, Mommy didn't get your doggie yet, precious," she said, kissing Elisha all over her face. She noticed her mother standing in the doorway. "Mom, did you lose some weight or something?" Melinda asked.

"Or something? Either you think I did or I've got more work to do." Mrs. Robinson smiled. "How was your trip?"

"It was so much fun! There were so many people skiing, networking, and partying. I think there were about seven thousand or so people from all over the U.S. sliding through Vail. We looked like a bunch of onyx jewels parlaying the white powder," she said.

"Really? Did they happen to have some type of church service available for all the repenting I know all you seven thousand needed?" Mrs. Robinson asked, raising her brow.

"Well, let me see. Naw, I don't think I remember seeing any flyers circulating for service. Actually I think everyone went to service before their vacation. You know, to sort of take out some repentance on credit?" Melinda teased.

"Girl, hush your mouth. Did you meet any prospects? You know, a nice Christian man like your daddy?"

"That depends, do you mean someone *just* like Daddy, age and all?" Her mother gave her a disapproving stare. "I'm just kidding you, Mom." She paused before she spoke again. "I did see Don."

"Don? You mean the nice fellow from Philly who you should have married?" Her mother leaned against the doorframe. "How's he doing? He's such a nice young man. Is he married? Got any kids?"

"Goodness, Mother, slow down. Yes, the Don Tolliver from Philly. No, he's not married, nor does he have any dependents, and he is doing just fine."

"Well, praise God for that," she mumbled. "Come on, Elisha," she called after the little girl. "We need to get ready for afternoon service 'cause Lord knows your mama is too tired to go."

Elisha held on to her mother's hand as she slid off the bed and stumbled over to her grandmother. Melinda, exhilarated by her mother's unyielding approval of Don, hopped out of bed and started preparing for her day. First, she would call Georgette and fill her in about her conversation with Don last night. Then, she would find out where the post-Super Bowl parties would be. She had missed half the game. She grasped the cordless phone and hit one of the memory keys.

"Georgette? Hey, girl, how you doing? Get any sleep last night?" giggled Melinda.

"Hey, girl. Sleep? Hardly. Gerard picked me up from the airport and one thing led to another."

"Uh-hum. Georgette, you will not believe it. After I got in last night, I spoke to Don for almost three hours. Georgette, it's so good to talk to him again. It's sounding pretty serious."

"Get outta here. Already? He must have laid it on pretty thick."

"Yeah, well, he laid it on thick and I smoothed it over easy. Anyway, how things go with you and Gerard? Did he at least pick you up on time?"

"Heck, no, and to be honest I don't know how things are, really. Last night he told me that he got accepted to Rutgers Law School on a partial scholarship and that we may need to postpone the wedding."

"What?" shouted Melinda. "He wants to do what? Excuse me, but, like, people aren't married and attending law school? Ain't that some . . . After all you have been through with his tired ass, that's it? 'Let's just postpone the wedding for a while my *chérie amour* so I can go to law school'? Is he retarded?"

"Yo, Melinda, calm down, okay? I know you can't stand Gerard, that's quite obvious, but he says it may be only for a year."

"Yeah, right," murmured Melinda over a click on the phone.

"Hold on, hotpants, it's my other line."

"Okay," Melinda pouted. Melinda hated Gerard. She disliked him long before he started dogging her girl. The first time she met him he had said something distasteful to her regarding her dark complexion. "Oh, you one of them charcoal mamas," she remembered his punk ass saying when no one was around to hear. Georgette can do a whole lot better. She's wasted enough clock with this overachieving, obnoxious watermelon head.

"Melinda, guess who that is on the other line?"

"Who?"

"It's Ray." Melinda could feel Georgette's smile over the phone.

"Well, go, girl, tell him I said hi. I'll talk to you a little later."

"Okay, I will. And Melinda? Thanks for being a friend. A motherly one but a good one nonetheless."

"Yeah, yeah. Love you, too, Georgette."

Georgette clicked back to Ray. "Ray, you there?"

"Right here, babe."

"So how was your flight home?" Georgette asked a little breathlessly.

"Long, but I slept all the way. I really don't like flying."

"You think that's a long flight? Try adding a couple of more hours to Philly," she said.

"Well, since I can't do the Denver to Philly flight to really understand where you're coming from, I guess I'll have to gauge it from Chicago to Philly, huh?" he laughed.

"Yes, I guess you'll have to, won't you?" Georgette wrapped the phone cord around her manicured nail.

"I have a very dear cousin that lives in Philly. Maybe I'll give her a call and try to come out that way in the near future. How would you feel about that?"

"Just how near are we talking?" she asked, laughing. "Ray, you know I would love for you to visit Philly." An image of Gerard faded out of her mind.

"If I came it would probably be in the next month or two. I have a convention coming up soon in New York, but I need to check and see when it is for sure. Would that be good for you?" he asked.

"Are you planning to stay with your cousin?"

"Oh, of course, Georgette. I hope I didn't imply—"

"No, you didn't, but I needed to be clear up front, you know?"

"My coming out there won't cause a lot of flack for you and homey, will it?" he asked.

"Why would you ask that?" she said, swallowing heavily.

"Because I noticed the ring you were wearing and all, but I didn't know if you lived together or if, well, you know."

"We don't shack together, Ray, no. I have my own abode. Furthermore, do you think I would have given you my number if I was living with someone?"

"You've got a point. But so many couples are so liberal in their relationships nowadays, I just didn't know how to take things," he said.

"I can assure you that I'm not that liberal. Openly share my man? I think not!" she said.

"But how would he feel about you striking up a new relationship with a stranger that happens to be of the same gender as him? Would he go for that?"

"Let's not get into that, if you don't mind. Bottom line is, I am very capable of making my own choices. Okay?"

"Okay, then. Listen, I don't want to keep you on the phone all day. I know you're probably watching the Super Bowl," he said.

"Yeah, how about this game. What's up

with these AFC teams? Wait, don't tell me you're rooting for the AFC," she teased.

"Sort of," he sighed. "It's a shame to see them lose so many years in a row. Besides, what you doing rooting for the NFC, anyway? Aren't you an Eagle's fan?"

"Yes, but the Eagles are a part of the NFC. . . . You know, the NFC East Division that represents the epitome of how the game is to be played?" She laughed.

"Oh, here we go with that East Coast blah, blah, blah. I don't recall Philly making it to the Super Bowl anytime during my lifetime."

"All right now, let's not ruin a good thing."

"Seriously, Georgette. I think it's cool the way you enjoy sports."

"I'm glad somebody does. Nobody else around here appreciates me. We better get going. I'm sure the AFC team is making a gigantic comeback and I definitely wouldn't want you to miss it."

"Ha, ha, ha, very funny. I'll call you later this week after I speak to Lynn. I'm looking forward to seeing you, as well as to that home-cooked meal you're gonna make for me. Oh, don't get quiet on a brother now. The way I see it, I'm sure whipping up some collards, macaroni and cheese, smothered chicken, and a chocolate cake can't be as challenging as maintaining the stats on some washed-up team like the Eagles."

"We will just have to see, won't we? All right, then, Mr. Fuschée, good talking to you. And Ray?"

"Yes?"

"Go Bills!"

Georgette noticed her beaming face reflected in the bathroom mirror. She realized how much she liked and even missed Ray. Holding the curling iron in one hand, she smoothed over one side of her hair. Impressing Gerard was her priority for the moment, she reminded herself. Feeling drained from the flight and her wild evening with Gerard, she collapsed on the sofa, drifting in and out of the Super Bowl action on the screen.

Gerard is up to something, she thought. She could sense it. She hoped and prayed that he wasn't sneaking around again. She would slay him if she found out. Especially if he's messing around with that witch Cheryl. She couldn't understand why Cheryl wanted to be with a man she knew had a woman. Cheryl had done the same crap to Melinda a few years ago. Befriending Don during their breakup just to get close to him, to hurt Melinda and to piss Georgette off. Cheryl's been after Gerard since she could remember. All Georgette knew was that she had better keep her distance or she would be sorry. No more Ms. Nice Girl. She was tired of people playing games and disrespecting her. To let the truth be known, Gerard and Cheryl probably deserved each other. They cared only about their self-gratification and they don't care at whose expense. To top it off, they both think they're God's gift to men and women. Cheryl parading around half naked all the time, boobs hanging out, ass hanging out, pretending to be so damn incapable of doing anything without the assistance of a man. The real deal was Georgette loathed Cheryl. The mere mention of her name could generate the breakout of a skin rash. She couldn't stand being in the same room with her let alone the same sorority. Lord forgive her, but if Cheryl were to drop dead today it wouldn't be soon enough. The jingle of the phone put a stop to her thoughts.

"Hello."

"NFC is best!" screamed the voice on the other line.

"Hey, Gerard," she mumbled.

"Wow, don't sound so excited. I just wanted to tell you I would be a little late."

"How late, Gerard?"

"I don't know, maybe a couple of hours."

"A couple of hours? Why?" she smirked.

"Some of the bros and I want to swing by this Super Bowl post-party to celebrate the victory."

"Oh, and I'm supposed to wait around until you decide it's time to show up for your date? You're already a couple hours late."

"Aw, Georgette, please! It's only for a couple of hours. You act like it's a damn eternity."

"You know what, Gerard? I tell you what. You be here in the next, let's say, thirty minutes like you're supposed to be. Or you can just do some friendly boodie banging with your frat brothers the rest of your life, understand?"

"Girl, you have truly flipped!" There was an intense pause on the line for a minute. Finally Gerard broke the silence. "I'll be there when I can."

"Yeah, well, you do what you must do, Mr. Man, 'cause like I said, I will be available until nine forty-five. It's now nine-fifteen."

"Yeah, whatever," Gerard mumbled, crashing the phone in her ear.

This Negro has lost his mind. First, he jumped up at the crack of dawn pretending to have some fraternity business to attend. Then, he promises to come over around halftime so that they could watch the Super Bowl together and go to dinner afterwards. Then it was "I'll be over right after the game." Now, he expects to come by *a couple of hours* after the game. No way! she thought to herself, I will make myself unavailable if he does show up. I don't know why he insists on gaming with me. He should realize by now he can't win. She was so angry she could have spit fire. The telephone's renewed ringing startled her.

"Yes," she said, exhaling a deep breath as she snatched up the phone.

"Hey, gorgeous," the deep voice said on the other end.

"Who is this?"

"It's Ray. Did I reach you at a bad time?"

"No, not at all. It's fine."

"I guess you were right about the NFC East," he said.

"Did you believe otherwise?" she questioned.

"I didn't think you would be home. I was going to leave a little message."

"What kind of message?"

"You'll just have to wait and hear it next time. How come you're not out celebrating?"

"It's a long involved but unimportant story. Besides, it's getting pretty late here on the East Coast."

"Oh, I see, can't hang on the coast but can wear somebody out on the slopes." He laughed. "I really enjoyed your company and your skiing abilities," he continued.

"Really?"

"Sure! It's not often that a brother meets a beautiful sister who is a semi-pro on the slopes and an avid, knowledgeable football fan."

"*Semi*-pro? Yeah, okay. I got your semi-pro for you the next time we hit the powder. To be honest, I was impressed with your skiing abilities as well. And I enjoyed your company as well as your gentle nature," she teased.

"I can be real gentle," he whispered.

"Oh is that right?" she asked.

"Mmmhmm. It's real easy being so caring and so gentle toward someone I view as special."

"Special, huh?"

"Yeah. Special."

Before Georgette knew it, time had flown by. She had switched from the cordless to the phone in her bedroom and lay across the bed talking, fantasizing, smiling, laughing endlessly with the charming man on the receiving end. It didn't seem to bother her that the clock struck twelve and her so-called prince had not arrived. She was engaged, intertwined with a king. A handsome, witty, intriguing brother named Ray.

Maybe her prince was the one trying to beep in on the other line, but she didn't feel compelled to find out. Ray's persona was magnificent and powerful. His words deliberate and direct. She could detect his passion for life and for her through the fiber optics. She wished they were still blazing down the white-covered mountains of Vail and that she was still lost in his embrace.

After the conversation, she lay awake staring at the ceiling, thinking hard about the man who had captivated her mind and part of her heart. This is crazy, she vowed. Could it be infatuation? Could it be lust? She quickly dismissed the lust factor, taking into account that her relationship with Gerard was not lacking in that area, but she couldn't help but wonder what it would be like to be with Ray.

The doorbell's buzz brought her rudely out of her reverie. Who in the world could it be at this hour? It better not be Gerard, she thought. Peeping out the corner of the living room blinds, she saw the beemer parked in the driveway. Now he is truly tripping, coming over here at twelve-thirty laying on the bell. "What do you want, Gerard?" she drilled through the cracked door.

"Where the hell have you been?" he demanded, pushing his way inside.

"What?" she snapped back.

"I said, where have you been?"

"Where have *you* been?" she replied.

"Look, Georgette. I told you I would be here later on. I tried to call you twice and got no answer. So I will ask you again, where have you been?"

"I've been right here doing things," she said.

"Things like what?"

"Things, okay? Besides, why are you getting all increased systolic over diastolic on me? Your butt was supposed to be here at nine forty-five!"

"Well, I called at nine-fifty and didn't get an answer."

"That's bull, Gerard. You didn't call till ten-fifteen the first time and eleven-thirty the second time."

"How did you know it was me? I didn't leave a message and your answering machine didn't pick up. Oh, let me guess. You were on the phone with that friend of yours, Melinda?"

"Yeah, I was on the phone, and no it wasn't with my best friend in the whole universe Melinda."

"Then who were you on the phone with that you couldn't answer my calls?" he snarled.

"Don't you worry about it. You weren't worried about it earlier while you were out and about doing your thing."

"Georgette, I swear to God one of these days you're going to push me to the point of doing something you will regret!"

"Oh please!" she said exasperatedly, brushing past him toward the kitchen.

"So who were you talking to?" he asked, following behind her.

"It's not important to you," she answered.

Gerard felt the anger brewing. Before he knew it, he had snatched her by the arm and flung her around to face him. The surprised look on her face was somewhat gratifying to him. He had smelled fear before from the

pledgees on line but never from Georgette.
He couldn't help but feel victorious. Surely
she would now instinctively confess who she
had been on the phone with. But then her
widened eyes began to squint. He could feel
her rage like daggers from her eyes. "Oh
shit," he murmured, just as her small hand
skidded across his face.

"Let me go, Gerard, now!" she screamed.
Before long, they were both hitting the floor
and scrambling wildly to break from each
other's grip. Georgette was out of control,
kicking and swinging furiously. Gerard covered his vitals, waiting for the fit to subside.
How did it get to this? he thought, rising to
his feet. *How?* He began heading toward the
door. Feeling Georgette closing the gap behind him, he turned to face her. Her hair was
all over her head and her face red as a beet
as she glared at him. Finally, she reached for
her left ring finger. She glided the ring off
in one stroke. "Here!" she said, throwing the
ring at him as she passed him to open the
front door. Long tears were streaming down
her face. "Get out!" she ordered.

It took a moment for Gerard to digest what
was happening. Still dazed by her anger, he
hung his head and attempted to speak.
"Georgette, I—"

"Just leave Gerard."

He tried to give her the ring back but she
wouldn't unfold her arms. He gave her a

pleading look but still she didn't budge. Slowly walking past her, he felt her nudge him out the door. The force created by the slam made him jump. *What had just happened? What had he just done?*

Gerard sat in his car paralyzed. Why was he so upset, so enraged with the answers she gave him? He still couldn't understand why she wouldn't tell him who she had been on the phone with. Still foggy, he backed out of the driveway, dipping the front tire over the curb. The car accelerated as he drove down the lonely street. How the heck did they hit the floor? He replayed the scenario over and over, searching desperately for an acceptable answer. The high was gone, the epinephrine rush subsiding now. He felt a stinging across his cheek. "I can't believe she slapped me," he muttered. "Why did she give back the ring?"

It seemed like he had been driving forever when he finally reached his garage. The night mirrored his feelings; dark, cold, desolate. His hands were still trembling as he placed the key in the lock. Once inside, he flopped down on the suede love seat. Clasping the cellular phone, he attempted to dial Georgette's number but his fingers wouldn't cooperate. Why had she acted so deranged? Why the exhaustive effort to hand back the ring? There were too many factors to consider. *Was he wrong for questioning her?* He

pondered the question long and hard until
the phone rang. He moved to answer it. It
was probably Georgette calling back to apologize. He would make her work hard for it,
he decided.

"Yeah," he said weakly.

"Gerard, are you sleep?"

He sighed heavily. "No," he muttered,
slouching back against the sofa. He had
flicked the TV on and was flipping through
the channels unconsciously.

"You sound upset."

There was a lengthy pause as he took a
deep breath, then let it go. "Yes, I am," he
said.

"Want to talk on the phone or do you want
me to come over there?" asked the female
voice on the other line.

"Whatever. It doesn't even matter."

"Okay, then, I'm on my way," she said.
"Gerard?"

"Yes?" he snapped.

"Have you eaten?" she asked.

"Yes, Cheryl, I have; and no, I'm not hungry."

"Then I'll see you soon."

Ten

"Hey, girl, are you on the other line?"

"Georgette? What's wrong?"

"I . . . I just need someone to talk to, that's all."

"Hold on, let me get off the line with Don, okay?"

"No, that's all right, Melinda. Just call me when you're done," Georgette said.

"No! Hold on. You sound upset. Wait a minute. I'll be right back."

Georgette began questioning why she had called Melinda in the first place. Yeah, she was her best friend, but she also didn't care for Gerard. Maybe she wouldn't tell her everything. She would say they had an argument instead of a fight.

"Girl, what's wrong? You sound horrible." Melinda always had the tendency to add a touch of dramatics to any situation.

"I don't even know where to start," Georgette said.

"Well, are you hurt or what?" Melinda asked.

"Mentally? Physically? Yes."

"Look, Georgette, you're scaring me. What's wrong?"

"Gerard and I had a fight," she blurted out.

"What kind of fight? A physical one?" Melinda asked, shocked.

"Yeah, sort of."

"What the hell do you mean, sort of? Did he hit you?" demanded Melinda.

"Melinda, it happened so fast I can barely remember. All I know is he snatched me by the arm and all hell broke loose."

"What? Georgette, did he hit you? Did he?"

"No, Melinda, please."

Melinda could hear the lump building up in Georgette's throat. "I'm sorry Georgette. Are you sure you're going to be okay? Do you need medical attention or anything?"

"No, I'm fine. Just a little shook up, that's all."

Georgette continued with the story blow by blow, pausing occasionally to gasp for air between the light sobs. After speaking with Melinda, she felt a little lighter, surprised even at how supportive Melinda had been and how removed she was from dogging Gerard out completely. What had caused all this upheaval anyway? Georgette did not have a clue. All she knew for sure was her aching heart and the lightness of her left finger that once displayed a bond between two people. A bond shared with her and Gerard. Now what? What would she tell her relatives? Her friends? Her co-workers? Why did she care, anyhow? He was wrong for grabbing her the way he did to begin with. Surely he couldn't have been serious about who she had been on the phone with when he was wrong from jump, hanging out with his frat all day and all night breaking dates. "Damn it all!" she frowned, rolling over to sleep. "I've gotta get some rest. I've got a job to go to tomorrow."

Gerard despised the corporate system when it came to Mondays. He figured people should be able to pick and choose which days of the week they wanted to work. By choosing what days to work, people might be more productive. On the other hand, anarchy would more than likely be the ultimate end result. Mondays seemed so dreary, so slow. People drove slow, walked slow, and reacted slow. His Monday morning blues almost cost him a new fender as he pulled the beemer into space number sixty-four.

"What's up, G?" Tyrone said, giving Gerard the fraternity handshake. Tyrone was dressed in a tailored olive green two-piece suit that hung neatly from his six-foot-three-inch frame. His attaché case was in his left hand and his trench coat draped over his left forearm.

"Hey Tyrone, what's happening?" Gerard replied, dropping his key chain into his burgundy leather briefcase.

"You tell me, man. You're the one looking like you had the overactive weekend," Tyrone laughed. He had a soft voice for a tall man who weighed in at 225 pounds. It was obvious to most people that Tyrone was from a mixed marriage. His father, a black man, and his mother, a Filipino, were responsible for his smooth mocha complexion, wavy jet black hair, heavy eyebrows, and unique eyes.

"Yeah? Well, you don't know the half of it."

"Oh, I don't know about that. The way you look I'd bet you either had a stressful weekend or you pumped a little too much."

"Humph. That's funny, Ty. Actually, Friday and Saturday were fine. Yesterday was a disaster."

"Really? It didn't seem too disastrous to me. I saw Cheryl's RX7 parked in front of the crib when I got home last night."

"Man, don't raise them doggone Herman Monster eyebrows at me. Besides, it ain't all of that," Gerard said.

"Yeah, right, that's why you been sneaking around with her. How's Georgette?"

"That witch," Gerard said under his breath.

"Dag, man, it's like that?"

"Hell, yeah, it's like that."

"What she do, man?"

"I really don't feel like getting into it. All you need to know is that Cheryl will be attending the Purple and Gold Ball with me. So you might want to give Vanessa the news on what's up so she won't be expecting her favorite soror, Georgette."

"All right, man. If you need an ear, stop by with some Moosehead and I might be persuaded."

"You mean some Coronas?" laughed Gerard.

"Whatever, frat, you know where to find me."

"Later, man."

"Peace."

Gerard headed toward the elevators marked for floors fifteen through thirty. Tyrone veered for the elevators marked thirty-one to forty-five. It was cool the way they met. Gerard had come in one Saturday to do some extra work. Tyrone noticed the Omega hat and greeted him as a fellow frat. They had remained aces ever since.

"Good morning, Mr. Jenkins," smiled the receptionist as Gerard entered the lobby.

"Good morning, Vivian."

"How was your weekend?" she asked.

"Oh, it was just that, an end of a week. Any messages?"

"Yes. Let's see, one from a Ms. C. L. Gray. She said to give her a call when you get in."

"Thanks Vivian." He strolled into his office, checking to make sure everything was in place.

Cheryl didn't waste any time jumping on the scene. She had just left him a few hours ago and now she was calling first thing. Maybe he shouldn't have told her about the fight. He really hoped that she wasn't relapsing into one of her sweating-him stages. Calling all the time, dropping by unannounced. His eyes gazed out the seventeenth-story window. *Philly is a dingy city,* he thought. How he would love to move somewhere where the grass invaded every inch of space. Moving to Jersey to attend Rutgers Law wouldn't be any better, with all the pollution and toxic waste, he thought.

He found himself thinking about Georgette and what she might be telling all her cronies and sorors. "Screw it," he dismissed aloud. If she wants me she knows where to find me. The buzzer to his intercom brought him out of his thoughts.

"Mr. Jenkins, there is a call for you on line one."

"Who is it?"

"She wouldn't give her name." For a quick moment his heart skipped, then leaped. He hoped it was Georgette.

"Yes, this is Gerard."

"Hey, baby, how's your back?" asked the voice on the other end.

"Cheryl? Hey, let me ring you back. I just walked in and I have some pressing things to take care of."

"All right, handsome. How's about lunch?"

"I'll get back to you in a few and let you know," he promised, hanging up the phone.

He had no intention of getting back to her about lunch, any more than he had pressing matters to attend to. He needed to delve back into his trance for a few more minutes. To daydream about Georgette and what was really going on with her. She had never acted this way before. Not even after she found out about Cheryl. She was up to something, but what? Why? She couldn't have known about Cheryl. It was just that one time, besides last night, that he had messed with Cheryl since their reconciliation.

He thought about the trip to Jamaica they were supposed to take this spring. About the five-thousand-dollar mink coat; the one-thousand-dollar ski gear and the four-thousand-dollar rock he just purchased. All this within a three-month period. Not that the money was ever the issue. Gerard's Christmas bonus was five thousand dollars, in addition to his regular end-of-the-year bonus which totaled a whopping twelve thou. No, it wasn't the money. He was just startled at the way Georgette had disrespected him. He purchased her everything she whined for, pleaded for, or simply expressed a desire for. Certainly the loving wasn't the problem. She never complained before, and she couldn't have been faking all the time. Maybe it was the time or lack of time he shared with her. Maybe he was feeling guilty for no reason. Or, perhaps he *had* a good reason. But whatever the cause was, he didn't feel that he owed her a damn apology. He didn't do anything wrong. He simply asked her a question, who was she talking to? The thought obsessed him as he reached for the yellow pages, he needed to place a call. Maybe, just maybe, he was wrong.

The phones were ringing out of control when Georgette arrived late to work. She had overslept after forgetting to reset her alarm. Preoccupied with the temporary chaotic state of the office, she hadn't noticed the enormous floral arrangement cascading over her desk. Immediately she felt nervous. Gerard had only sent her flowers on one other occasion and that was after she'd exposed his affair with Cheryl. Last night's episode was a whole lot worse. He could have at least called to speak with her first before purchasing the flowers. *What a weak way out*, she thought. At any rate, they were a beautiful arrangement of red, purple, and yellow gladioluses. She wondered why Gerard didn't send them more frequently. Maybe he didn't know how much she loved flowers.

Hesitantly, she walked over to the arrangement and picked up the card. It read *Special* on the outside. She opened it. *Hope you're having a blessed and prosperous day. Stay sweet, Ray.* She couldn't help but smile. How thoughtful of him. Gosh, how she always dreamed of a man sending flowers to her job or home for no reason whatsoever. She noticed the jitters fading. "I should have known it was too good to be true," she whispered. Flowers from Gerard—what was she thinking?

"Georgette, you have a call on hold," her secretary said.

"Who is it?" Georgette asked.

"A woman. She didn't give her name."

"Probably Melinda. Thanks Anne." By the time she picked up the line, there was nothing but a dial tone at the other end. Georgette reset the phone in order to place a call to Melinda. She probably just wanted to know how she was doing.

"Ms. Robinson please," requested Georgette.

"This is Melinda."

"Hey."

"Hey, Georgette. How you feeling today?"

"A little better. I'm still a little dazed, but guess what? Ray sent me flowers."

"Girl, this man is in love. Did you call him yet?"

"Not yet, but I will. Melinda, I can't believe how fast things are moving between us. Last year this time you would have never been able to convince me that, this time this year, my heart would be flipping and flopping for another man so quickly. It's kind of scary for me. I feel like I'm floating in outer space. After all, we only spent a week together and already he's talking about trying to develop a long-distance relationship. How come I feel so comfortable and secure with him? What do you think Melinda?

"I think it's great! Don't read too much into everything. Besides, if you spend too much time trying to evaluate the situation, you're liable to sabotage the relationship. Let go, relax, keep your head about you and watch his actions. Okay?"

"Okay. Hey, did you just call me a few minutes ago?"

"Nope, it wasn't me," Melinda said.

"I wonder who it was then. Anne said she didn't give her name. And she knows my mom and my sister. I thought it might have been you."

"Afraid not. Anyway, I would have given my name."

"Well, whoever it was will have to call back if it's important. I'll call you a little later and let you know how I'm feeling. I also want to tell you about my conversation with Ray last night," she finished with a giggle in her voice.

"Okay. Call me after eight. I have step class tonight. By the by, I might be in Philly next weekend."

"Oh really? To do what?" teased Georgette.

"What do you think, girlfriend? To see you, of course," Melinda joked.

"Yeah, right."

"Well, Don invited me down for his birthday weekend and I accepted," Melinda answered.

"Oh, I see. A little birthday celebration with the one you love?"

"Love? Well, yeah, you could say that. I'll call you later. I gotta go."

Georgette thought about who the mysterious caller had been. Only a few people had her work number. Why did this mystery lady decline to leave her name? Sounded strange, but she didn't want to worry about it. Then it struck her. The last time some woman had called anonymously, it turned out to be Cheryl harassing her about Gerard. Imagine that, Cheryl calling her at her place of work to argue. At first Georgette couldn't figure out how Cheryl got her work number. But then she recalled that her work and home numbers were listed in the sorority's phone book. Suddenly she felt queasy. Why would

Cheryl be calling about Gerard? He couldn't
have jumped back into her arms that quickly.
Who knows and who cares, she forced herself
to think. She can't trust him anyway. She had
no business accepting his proposal. *Why have
I wasted so many years trying to change Gerard,
trying to make him be who and what I want him
to be?* She had thought love could conquer
all.

Georgette decided she would drop a card
in the mail to Ray at lunchtime and give him
a call later. It was thoughtful of him to send
flowers. How bizarre having someone tuned
into you so swiftly. She found herself day-
dreaming about Ray a lot since her return
from Vail. There was something about him
for sure. The buzz of the phone interrupted
her thoughts.

"Phone call for you Georgette," Anne announced. "Sounds like the same woman that
called earlier."

"Okay, put her through. This is Georgette." There was a pause for a moment,
then a voice erupted.

"Georgette, why don't you just let Gerard
go?"

"Who is this?" she asked, but she could
tell it was Cheryl.

"Don't worry about that! What you need
to worry about is getting on with your life.
It's apparent he's getting on with his!" The
voice was sharp and strident.

"Is that right? Well, then, I suppose you should be getting on with your life as well and quit calling folks at work."

"Ah, f you Georgette. You ain't nothing but a spoiled, weak, unappreciative . . ."

"You know what, Cheryl? I would love to hang out with you on the phone the rest of the afternoon, but I really have something that is just a little bit more important to do than discussing Gerard with you. Why don't you make an appointment with my secretary to come on down to my office so we can settle this matter face to face, once and for all?"

Georgette could hear Cheryl huffing on the other end of the phone. There was a long pause, before Georgette said, "I didn't think so," as she hung up.

Click! Georgette's adrenaline had kicked in, switching from fifth gear into third without any warning or advance notice. What is going on around here? First Gerard last night and now Cheryl. "I cannot believe this," she grumbled while dialing the phone.

"Melinda please," she heard herself say.

"This is Melinda."

"I swear, if hell is anything like these last twenty-four hours, I'm tying up my stuff to ensure my residence in heaven."

"What could have happened since I last spoke to you?" asked Melinda.

"Cheryl just called me here at the job."

"Girl, shut up! You serious?"

"What, you think I'm not? I just hung up on her. Can you believe that?"

"Georgette, I don't know about you."

"Me! What have I done?"

"Relax. I'm just saying if it ain't Gerard tripping with you, it's his part-time freak tripping with you. You need to drop his behind for sure, do you hear me?"

"Yeah I hear you, but Melinda why? Why is this other woman calling me? Isn't it bad enough he's obviously still messing around with her while supposedly engaged to me?"

"Well, I'm not going to say too much because you know how I feel about Gerard."

"Yup, but I'm still perplexed. How could he do this and so soon? I don't know, Melinda. I feel like such a sucker. Do you think he ever really loved me?"

"Does it really matter? Don't do this to yourself, okay? I won't be in Philly until next weekend. Tell you what, why don't you come up to New York tonight? It will take your mind off things. You've got enough vacation days stored. How about it?"

"Thanks, but I'll be fine. I just need to do some soul-searching, you know? I'm feeling a bit shattered."

"Are you sure, Georgette?"

"Yeah."

"Call me if you change your mind. I'll be right here."

"Thanks Melinda. Love you."

"Love you, too."

Georgette sat at her desk, staring out of her office window. Maybe she *should* ride up to New York tonight. Or maybe she should go to Bible study instead. It had been a few weeks since she last attended any service. It sure would give her the boost she needed. But she didn't feel much like sermons either. What she really wanted was for Gerard to call her and apologize. Tell her that he still loved her and that things could possibly work out. Or maybe he would drive by and drop the ring off with some flowers. She released a heavy sigh, wishful thinking on her part. Her best bet would be to attend Bible study tonight. Yeah, that's what it'll be. Her and the Lord tonight.

Eleven

"Please leave a message after the beep . . ."

"Lynn, this your cousin Ray. Long time, no hear. Give me a call when you get in. I'm thinking about visiting your neck of the woods in a few weeks so buzz me. Oh, by the way, I like your message. Who is that in the background, Boys II Men? Call me."

Ray wanted to call Georgette and see whether or not she received the flowers. *I can't be too anxious,* he thought. He didn't want her to think he was pressuring her or anything. The small black receiver cupped in his hand began to vibrate even before the ringing started. Maybe this was Georgette now.

"Hello?"

"Ray? Is that you?"

"Hey, cuz, is that you?" he asked.

"It's me, alive and well," she said.

"Hey, girl, what's up? I just left you a message not even two minutes ago."

"Yeah, I know, but I couldn't catch the call so I had to wait for it to go to the voice mail, before I could call you back. So, what's been up? We haven't talked in what—three, four months?"

"Try five or six months. Everything is going just grand with me. I've been working a lot of hours as usual, but it finally paid off. I got promoted to lieutenant."

"Congratulations! Lieutenant Ray, way to go! So, how's Anthony doing?"

"He's fine, getting big as a boat. I'm going to have to pick up a second job just to feed that boy," he laughed.

"Yeah, well, raising children nowadays is certainly a costly endeavor, both financially and physically."

"Who you telling? I spend about three hundred dollars a month in child support and another one hundred fifty when he's with me. So tell me, when are you planning to have some crumbsnatchers?"

"Please! I'll do good to baby-sit the one you have. I don't know what's wrong with me, cuz, but I don't feel maternal in the least bit. In fact, I don't know what I would do if I got pregnant. Awh! Just the thought of it makes me ill." She laughed.

"Lynn, you shouldn't feel like something is wrong with you just because you don't want children. A lot of women are passing on the supposed blessed event. Just be lucky you have a wonderful cousin residing in Chicago who would be glad to share his child with you whenever you want. Summers, winters, hell, all year round if you want." He laughed.

"I'm sure Ms. Rachel would just love that, wouldn't she? How are you doing? You know, with the divorce, Anthony, and all?"

"I'm hanging. There's really not too much I can do. But I do know I don't miss being married to her at all. In fact, I finally realized how much more of an obligation it was on my part than an act of happiness. I was miserable, trying to do the right thing for the sake of everyone else instead of me. I'm glad it's over. I'm just sorry that Anthony has to deal with the broken home syndrome, but I will do everything in my power to ensure that he has a stable, secure, healthy environment."

"I know you will, sweetheart. Nowadays, there are several brothers raising their children. I only wish there were more men in the world like you, I swear I do. Or, I wish you weren't my cousin, maybe then I could be the next Mrs. Fuschée. You're one of a kind, Ray. I don't know what I'd do without you. I love you, you know that, don't you?"

"Yes, I do know that, and I love you, too. How's your love life been? You find Mr. Right yet?"

"Perhaps, but I'm still working on him. Let's not talk about that now. Sounds like I might have an opportunity to update you in person. When are you planning to come to Philly?" she asked.

"I'm not sure yet. I know that I'll be in New York for a convention in a few weeks and I figured I'd jump on the train and head down there to visit you and a friend or two."

"Cool, you know my door is always cracked for you," she teased.

"What do you mean, cracked? I thought the saying was opened."

"Cracked, open, it's all a matter of perception. If the opportunity is availed even slightly, then it's up to each individual to see their way through, right?"

"Lynn, I gotta hand it to you. You still haven't lost your philosophical edge. Anyway, I'll call you in about two weeks to let you know exactly what my plans are, okay?"

"All right, you be careful putting out all them blazes, you hear me?"

"I hear ya. Thanks for being such a darling. See you soon."

Georgette immediately started smiling when she noticed the red Ford Bronco parked in front of her house. That was a smart thing she did a few months ago, giving her brother, Kyle, a key to her apartment. Entering the doorway, she could hear the top-forty station blaring from the speakers.

"Hey, Sis." A handsome young man with a brilliant smile greeted her.

"Hey, Kyle, what you doing here?"

"Waiting for my lovely sister to get home. So how was your ski trip?"

"It was great! I had a better time in one week than I did at half my college homecomings," she said.

"Oh yeah? Were there a lot of cutie-pies up there?"

"From a woman's perspective I have to say yes, hands down. There were a whole lot of us up there. In fact I got some pictures right here you can check out."

Georgette handed the pictures to Kyle to view while she looked through her mail. She always sat at the computer table when she opened her mail. It was the best place to file bills, throw away trash mail, and write out checks.

"Who is this girl?" he asked.

"Let me see," she said, summoning him over to the computer. "Oh, that's Jackie, a sorority sister from Oakland."

"Oakland, huh? Well, I might just have to make a little trip to Oak Town this summer. Is she married? Got a man? Gay? Looking for a good thang? What's up?"

"Boy, you crazy, you know that? Jackie is not married, never been married, and she is definitely not gay. She does have a son. That's him sitting right there," she pointed out.

"I think it's cool that she took him along with her and didn't dump him off while she went out playing," he said, staring further at the photo.

"It wouldn't bother you that she has a child by someone else?"

"Why should it? If she's taking care of the child, giving him love and morals and not abusing him, what difference does that make? Besides, it's really about how she is as a person. Whether she's whole or not, you know?"

"I guess so." She was impressed with her brother's attitude. "But what about having to deal with the baby's father? Wouldn't that bother you?"

"I'm speaking purely hypothetically, of course, because I really don't know this woman. But unless the baby's father would blatantly try to disrespect me, it wouldn't bother me. I might be concerned about her emotional link to her ex and whether or not she can move forward. That's what it's all about, you know? Moving forward, progressing as a unit in a positive way," he finished.

"Gosh, Kyle, you sound so smart. I can't wait to see the lucky woman who'll snatch you up," she teased.

"Well thanks," Kyle blushed. "How is my future punk brother-in-law Gerard doing?"

"Oh, Kyle, don't start." She looked away. "To be honest, we broke up last night."

"Again? What is this, the third or fourth time?" he laughed. "What was it over this time if you don't mind me asking."

"Let me put it to you this way. She's back."

"Who? That girl from a few months ago?"

"Yeah, that hussy. She had the nerve to call me at work today, can you believe that?"

"I knew I should have stuck my foot up his little butt the first day I met him, worthless . . ."

"Kyle, I really don't want to go into it," Georgette interrupted. "I feel gloomy as it is, okay?"

"Okay, but let me ask you something. Who broke it off?"

"I did," she admitted.

"Good! So now what? You're feeling unsure of your decision? You're beginning to question your actions because of this phone call?" he asked.

"The thing of it is, we just broke up last night and she's on his tip already. It stands to reason that I'm feeling a little unsure, uncertain about Gerard's professed love for me."

"Listen, Sis, you need to remember something. Don't allow anyone to snatch power from you regarding your well-being. You made a decision based on some emotions that were stirred up. Obviously at the time, you felt that your decision was justified.

"Now that this woman has called you, you're willing to, once again, hand over control of your feelings, well-being, and peace of mind to someone who doesn't deserve it. In fact, no one deserves to rob anyone of their happiness! Not me, not Mom, Dad, Sis, Gerard, or this lady should handle or control your peace of mind and well-being. Let it rest and press on! You'll be just fine, girl. You know why? Because God never puts more on you than you can bear. That's what He told me in his word. Keep your head high, understand me, Georgette?"

"Thanks Kyle," she said, hugging him hard. "Thanks for the pep talk, I feel much better."

"You do? Then how's about you show it and take me out to dinner or whip up some of your famous smothered lamb chops." He laughed.

"You got it!" she smiled. "Actually, I was planning on going to Bible study. You want to go grab a bite to eat and then head to the church?"

"Bible study? Tell you what. Let's get a bite to eat and we can discuss the Bible on the way."

The phone rang just as they were leaving.

"Oh wait, let me grab that," Georgette said, rushing past her brother.

"Hello," she said.

" 'El-o, darling," the baritone voice echoed on the other end.

"Ray! Hi, how are you?" She looked to

Kyle, then turned her back for privacy. "Listen, I was going to call you later tonight to thank you for the flowers. They're beautiful."

"I was beginning to wonder. I didn't hear from you so I figured either they hadn't delivered them yet or you were allergic to them and you were just too sick to call." He laughed.

"No, I'm not allergic to any kind of flowers, so you need not worry. You don't know how much they lifted my spirits today."

"Good, that's what they were intended to do. Are you busy now?"

"My brother and I were just on our way out to grab a little snack and then head over to Bible study, right Kyle?"

Kyle mumbled a quick, "Yeah, yeah."

"I just wanted to let you know that I would be in New York for sure in the next couple of weeks and I was thinking of catching the train down to Philly to see the queen."

"I'd love to see you," Georgette said with a wide smile. "Tell you what, when I get back this evening I'll give you a call and we can go over the particulars, all right?" she said.

"Sounds good. Talk to you later."

By the look on Kyle's face, Georgette knew he was curious about Ray and that he would start grilling her at any moment.

"So, who's Ray?" he asked.

She kissed Kyle's cheek. "I'll tell you all about him on the way. Let's go!"

They jumped in the Bronco and sped off. Kyle believed in keeping the money in the country, that's why he purchased the Ford utility vehicle. Besides, he would never buy anything but American cars because he was just like her dad. She remembered her family having American cars all her life. They supported American stereos, too.

She didn't care about that sort of stuff, though. Her philosophy was, as long as the items worked and lasted forever, they were worth the money. Furthermore, the way she calculated, everything had some Japanese parts in it. It was like a virus, once it started it was hard to be rid of. She would have to find out Ray's view on buying American versus Japanese. Perhaps that would be something she would discuss with him later tonight. But who was she kidding? What she really wanted to know was his true intentions regarding their newfound friendship.

Twelve

The next several weeks passed uneventfully. Ray would be arriving in three days and she wanted her apartment to be in tip-top condition. She wasn't sure if he would end up staying with her or with his cousin Lynn. In either case, she wanted to make certain that her place was immaculate and cozy. That was only part of the reason.

The truth of the matter was that she had become a fanatic about housework since the breakup with Gerard. She didn't want to attend any functions for fear of bumping into Gerard and that witch Cheryl. Especially after hearing that they had attended the Purple and Gold Ball as a hot couple. That nearly broke her heart in half. How could he be so cold, openly marching around town with Cheryl? Yeah, it had been seven weeks since their breakup, but damn! He was back on the circuit in no time and strutting with a new honey on his arm. He and his frat brothers meeting with Cheryl and the other sorors down at the jazz festival in Jamaica the second weekend in March. It was like he was deliberately trying to stick it to her. He didn't even call her to wish her a happy birthday. She had rented a small room at a local restaurant to celebrate her birthday with a few close friends. She remembered blowing the candles out and thinking that Gerard could have at least acknowledged her birthday with a card or message on her answering machine.

For almost two months, she hadn't heard a thing from her ex-fiancé. Not even an apology. But that was all right, because now there was Ray to absorb some of her pain and burden.

Realizing her thoughts were too wrapped up in Gerard, she decided to give Dorian, her older, only sister, a call. It had been a while since she had had a long confiding conversation with her. Dorian had been swamped with her new practice and maintaining her home, as well as keeping a happy marriage with a husband who was also a physician with a heavy schedule.

"Hey, Dori."

"Hey, Georgette! How you doing?" her sister asked in her usual upbeat tone.

"Oh everything is everything, I guess," she said, sounding like Ray. This was his favorite line whenever she would ask him how he was doing.

"Is that my favorite sister-in-law?" she heard Phillip ask in the background.

"Phillip says hi."

"Tell him I said hello." Georgette paced her living room.

"What's wrong Georgi, you okay?"

"Yeah, I'm fine. Guess what? I'm expecting an out-of-town guest in a few days." She smiled.

"Really? And who might that be?"

"His name is Ray and I met him a few months ago at the ski summit. He's attending a convention in New York this week and he's coming to see me."

"Excuse me, Ms. Lady. We know things are over with you and Gerard but how come you never mentioned Ray before? Is he married or something?" Dorian asked.

"No, he's not married, at least not anymore. Furthermore, I know how protective you and Phillip can be so I decided to wait until I felt the timing was right," she said.

"I know what, why don't you guys come down to Virginia for the weekend so we can meet this Ray fellow?"

"Thanks, Dori, but he's only here for the weekend and I don't want to spend most of it on the highway."

"I understand. So, you said he's been married before?"

"Oh, here it comes . . ." Georgette plopped down on the couch.

"No. I'm asking, that's all. Does he have any kids?"

"One. A boy named Anthony who is three years old."

"Anthony, huh?"

"Yes, Anthony. And before you ask, Ray is a firefighter," she said.

"A firefighter, is that right? Where?"

"In Chicago."

"Well, I suppose there's a level of comfort in me not having to worry about losing you to a fire with him around. What's he bringing in, about forty g's?"

"You know Dori, not everyone can bring in six figures like you and Phillip."

"I don't know about that, Georgette. Gerard manages to do it all by himself."

"Oh, so now you're implying Gerard would be more acceptable because he makes more money? Is that what you're saying?"

"No, that's not what I'm saying! I'm just pointing out that once you get accustomed to a certain lifestyle it could be rather hard to make the adjustment to less. Does he have his bachelor's degree?"

"No, he doesn't. In fact, I don't think he even has his high school diploma. So now what do you think? You still want us to come down for the weekend?"

"Georgette, have you lost your mind?"

"No, I haven't lost my mind! But, I always try to deal with people based on who they are, not what they can provide for me," she snapped.

"Are you sure about that Georgi? What about the fur coat, the hundreds and hundreds of dollars worth of jewelry? Not to mention the paintings and even that rock you used to have on your finger. You have been acclimated to a particular lifestyle, are you sure you can let that go? That's all I'm asking?"

"I understand what you're trying to say and to a certain degree you have a valid point. I've thought about all of that. The fact that I may make a couple of thousand dollars more than him; the fact that he has a child already, an ex-wife; and the fact that he doesn't have a college degree. I've thought about it over and over. But frankly, I like him despite those things. He's a wonderful man. In any case, it's too soon for me to be assessing him as a future husband."

"Georgi, it is still food for thought. If they're issues now they will be issues later. Just beware and listen to your heart."

"I appreciate your concern, Dori, but there is something genuine about this brother. It's like I'm his queen; he respects me, you know? It's a nice feeling having someone express an unconditional interest in your well-being and happiness without trying to buy it."

"God knows I can relate. Phillip busted into the bathroom while the oatmeal mask was setting and the aroma of funk was oozing in the air and told me, baby, I love you. Girl, I wanted to crawl up under the toilet, the way I looked, but it felt good knowing no matter what I might look like or smell like, Phillip is in it for the long haul. Oops, my pager is flashing, I better call and see if one of my patients is having an emergency. Call me after the weekend and let me know how things turned out."

"I will. Talk to you later. Hugs and kisses."

"Hugs and kisses, little sis. God be with you."

The conversation with Dorian plus all the housework she had done wore Georgette out. She collapsed on her bed. How *would* she adjust to the change in status and clout? Gerard had never complained about finances. Even after purchasing the beach house on Martha's Vineyard last year, he still never missed a beat. Gerard's smooth like that, she thought. Ray's visit this weekend would tell it all. If he was strapped for cash she would find out soon enough. She planned a fun-filled weekend of events and restaurant escapades. If this brother was a cheapskate she certainly would find out now, before she invested too much more time and wishful thinking. At least she would get out of the house and back into the circuit for the weekend. In the groove with a handsome six-foot-three-inch chocolate brother. Hopefully she might even run into Gerard and his sidekick and show them she hadn't been beaten. That indeed this caramel-colored sister was back in action.

Thirteen

"So, I'll pick you up at the Thirtieth Street station. I'll be inside waiting for you."

"I'm so looking forward to seeing your pretty face in person. I was beginning to wear the videotape out from the ski summit. What's on the agenda for this evening?" Ray asked.

"I anticipate you might be slightly famished when you get here, so we'll probably stop by Strother's Cafe or Moody's on the Pike to replenish your strength. Do you like seafood?"

"Certainly do! That sounds delicious."

"Great! I'll see you in a few hours. We can figure out what else to do when you get here. Do you want to drop your things off at your cousin's house first?"

"Maybe. We'll play it by ear. She's not expecting me until sometime later this evening. I have the address tucked away in my wallet and the key she mailed me in case she wasn't home by the time I got there," he said.

"All right then, we'll decide when you get

here. I'll make the reservations for eight. See you soon."

Georgette's excitement raised a great deal of eyebrows at the office.

"What is going on with you, Georgette?" Anne questioned.

"Not too much. Only that Ray will be here tonight." She grinned.

"You better watch yourself this evening, Ms. Thing. In fact, I've got just the thing for you." Anne ruffled through her top desk drawer until she found the items. "Here. This is how you'll be able to tell just how swell Ray is," she said.

"Oh, Anne," Georgette said, taking the two condoms the woman held out.

"Read them. One is a Trojan large and one is a Magnum extra large. When it gets to that point, ask him which one he prefers. If he reaches for the Trojan you'll know what time it is. If he reaches for the Magnum you'll not only know what time it is in the good ole USA, you'll know what time it is all over the world," laughed Anne.

"Oh, I get it. That's pretty darn clever, Anne. But I don't think it'll come to anything like that this weekend. He's going to stay over at his cousin's place at least for tonight."

"Keep them anyway, just to be safe. Have a fun weekend. You are truly overdue."

"Thanks, Anne, you too. And don't worry,

I'll be fine. See you Monday. Maybe," she said with a wink. Georgette stuffed the condoms in her purse, snatched her briefcase, and headed toward the elevators. "This is going to be a phenomenal weekend!" she shouted through the crack of the closing elevator doors.

"Cheryl, what time are we supposed to hook up?"

"Dinner is at seven, Gerard. I told you that last night."

"I know, but the jet lag is catching up with me." He yawned.

"My goodness, Gerard, you only flew from Chicago. They're, what, one hour behind us? Maybe you need to lay off that social snorting. It will only lead you to an early grave. Aren't you worried about your job testing you?" Cheryl asked.

"This is Corporate America. They don't do that crap to the executives. Besides, I only do it every blue moon after I've had a hard meeting and a long flight. I can't wait until this deal in Chicago is complete. I'm getting rather burnt out from all the flying these past two weeks. The deal will probably close in the next two months for sure. What's for dinner tonight? Let's go out. How about the Phoenix? You feel like dancing?"

"Gerard, calm down, you're rambling and I can't keep up with you. I really wish you hadn't started sniffing that stuff again. Shoot! Look what time it is, I've gotta run. The bank closes in a half hour and I need to get some cash so I can pick up a few more things. Do you want wine or champagne with dinner?"

"I don't care, whatever you want. Let's plan on going out tonight, okay?"

"I've already planned on cooking a special meal," she whined.

"Really? Cool, then I'll be able to watch the game. You do get channel four, right?" He laughed.

"Ha, ha, very funny. You know good and well I get that channel. Listen, I need to go, I'll see you later. Oh, Gerard, I meant to—"

He hung up before she had a chance to finish. Her other line clicked in but she didn't have time to answer it. She would let the voice mail catch that call. She had a few errands to run.

Gerard ran to catch the elevators before they closed. He was glad that the weekend had arrived. The last three days in Chicago were hectic. He was trying to close a deal between a large bank in Chicago and his company, EPI. It would be a few more trips before they finalized everything. Jumping into the Jeep, he decided he better take care of a few errands himself.

First, he would stop by Bill's. The parking

lot was crowded as usual. Another thing he hated about Philly or metropolitan cities in general was the lack of parking spaces.

"Got a hot date tonight, Gerard?" Bill asked, greeting him at the front counter.

"You could say that. How's everything?"

"Fair to middlin'. All your stuff is ready except two of your shirts. Our starch mixture was a little hard so we had to remix it and do everybody's shirts over again. I can have Jimmy drop them off to you when they're ready," Bill offered. Everyone in the neighborhood took their clothes to Bill's. Mainly because his prices were a lot lower than most of the other cleaners in the area.

"No, that won't be necessary, Bill. I'll be in here next week to drop off some more clothes. I can wait until then. Hey, how's your grandson doing?"

"He's pulling through just fine. I betcha he'll keep his ass from around them Posse boys. If he don't, then he'll be getting a pine box next time instead of twenty-two stitches over an eye and a broken rib. How's them lady friends of yours?" chuckled Bill.

"Everyone is fine."

"Yeah? How about that real pretty brown-sugar sister who used to come in here to get your things? Ain't seen her around lately. How's she?"

"You mean Georgette? To be honest, I really don't know, Bill. We aren't together anymore." Gerard handed him two twenty-dollar bills. He was ready to split at the very mention of Georgette's name.

"She was a real nice young lady. You don't see too many of them around anymore. Heck, I can count how many men who has a young lady coming in here solely to pick up their clothes. Listen, Gerard, I know it's none of my business, but I've been around a lot longer than you so I'm going to say it anyway. Georgette was a special angel God gave to you. Don't mess around and let some devil of a woman rob you of your angel, or some other brother fly off with her. You hear?" Bill handed Gerard his change and looked once again into his eyes. "Be respectful, son. Be respectful."

Gerard flew out the door in a hurry. What's with everybody? he thought, placing the clothes on the backseat. First his mom and now Bill. He remembered vividly his mom's statement about Georgette. She pointed to him and said, "Gerard, Georgette is the wife God has ordained for you to have. Don't blow it messing around with some loosey-goosey." Everyone was on his case about Georgette. They will just have to accept that it's over between them, period. Bill was pretty slick the way he put a bug in his ear regarding Georgette and her wings flying off with some other man. She's not going to find anyone who would do the things that he did for her, anyway.

The way he saw it, if it weren't for him, she would still be sporting those passé designer jeans. Yeah, she's an angel all right, flying with the wings he bought for her. Let's see how well she'll be flying with one clipped one. Another man? Yeah, right. She's been undercover for almost two months licking her wounds.

She still had his other cellular phone that he wanted back. She never used the dang blasted thing anyhow. She might have tossed it in the trash by now just for spite, he thought. Naw, that's not fair to say. Georgette may be a lot of things, but spiteful wasn't one of them. That would be Cheryl. That's the one thing he admired about Georgette, the fact that she never stooped low. No, not ever. At least not until that night a few months ago. He still couldn't believe that all this had gone down just because he asked her a simple question. If Georgette wanted to piss him off, she sure did a good job by being so stubborn. The sounds of Kirk Whalum filled the car as Gerard navigated through the streets of Philadelphia.

It was one of Kirk's songs that drew Gerard to Georgette at one of the Greek picnics several years ago. She had whizzed by with some of her sorority sisters, laughing and flirting with the brothers as she passed by. Gerard noticed her honeysuckle skin beaming in the sun and the rays of soft brown and gold soft-crimp curls. She had her nails done in a French manicure overlaid with a pale peach color. She smelled good and looked good, too. But it was her eyes that had sealed his heart, those hazel eyes protected by those long curly lashes. When she opened her mouth to ask Gerard what his line name was, her teeth were perfectly straight and pearly. Her voice was low and seductive. After engaging him in conversation, he knew he had to be with her. Exuding intelligence, a great sense of humor, she captured a part of his soul and thus their story had evolved. He would be forever grateful to her for her support and love after his father's death. The way she stood by him day and night injecting her last bit of energy into him so that he could make it through another day. He would always love her for that. But, like every relationship, they had their share of problems. The ups, the downs, the arguments, the mistrust, the fun, the holidays, the lovemaking, the other women. They all had their place in the relationship. However, one of these things would inevitably be the demise, the death, of their journey together.

* * *

Cheryl had to complete her tasks before it got too late.

The first one would be quick. She needed to stop by the post office to mail Georgette a picture of her and Gerard. That'll fix her little ass for good, seeing the two of them together dressed to kill, arm in arm at the Purple and Gold Ball. Yeah, a little dab would do her, Cheryl thought to herself.

Georgette would probably figure out that she had sent the picture, but so what? She never wasted any time flaunting Gerard in her face so it serves her butt right. Cheryl mumbled under her breath, "I don't know who she thinks she is but when I do see her I'm going to slap the hell right out of her no matter where we are. She ain't nothing but a wimp anyway, too frightened to even show up at the last two sorority meetings. When she was with Gerard, we couldn't get enough of her jumping up and down at the meetings. Making grand entrances, strolling in late all the time with her fur coat swaying. God forgive me, but she is one woman I would pay to see put down on her face. She is too arrogant and stuck up. It doesn't matter, just as long as I have Gerard. Now let's see who's zooming who, Ms. Willis."

Parking the car in the handicap lane, Cheryl flipped on her hazards and darted into the post office. No one was inside so she went straight to the window.

"Will that be first class ma'am?"

"Yes, that'll be fine. Wait! How much is your overnight service?" Boy, she really wished she could be there to see Georgette's expression.

"It's nine ninety-five and it will be there by noon tomorrow. Do you wish to send it overnight instead? Miss? Miss, are you all right?" The postman became alarmed when the color starting draining from Cheryl's face and lips. When she began swaying backwards, as if her equilibrium was off, he started to make his way around the counter, but Cheryl stopped him, and seemed to regain her composure.

"I'm fine, thanks. Overnight will be fine." Cheryl took a deep breath. She was experiencing her second nausea spell. This was the fourth day in a row she had felt like passing out or throwing up. Oh God, she thought! She hoped she wasn't pregnant. She would have to stop by a store and purchase a home pregnancy test. Lord, she laughed, Gerard would burst an artery if she turned up pregnant.

The bank was crowded as usual. They needed to hire some more help or add an express line for customers with only one or two transactions, Cheryl thought, looking at her watch. She wanted to stop by the boutique to pick up her catsuit before they closed.

Then she could go home and lie down. The nausea was getting worse.

"I can help you here ma'am," the teller motioned.

"You guys are a little busy today," she said, handing him her slip.

"You can say that again. I need to see some I.D. please."

"I come here all the time," she said, reaching into her purse. She handed him her license.

"Nice picture," he smiled.

"Thanks."

"What would you like, twenties or fifties?"

"Fifties are fine."

"Here you go, Ms. C. L. Gray," the teller said with a flirty smile. "By the way, what does the L stand for?"

"Lynn. It's really a family name of sorts. Mostly everyone outside the family calls me Cheryl. But my full legal name is Cheryl Lynn Gray."

Fourteen

"What are you going to wear?" Melinda asked over the phone.

"I don't know. I was thinking about my green suede skirt and a nice silk blouse and my riding boots," Georgette answered.

"That sounds cute. You want to look sexy, but be warm at the same time. What perfume are you wearing?"

"Probably Carolina Herrera, that's my favorite. Girl, I'm so nervous. I hope all goes well."

"Georgette, things will be just fine. I think it's just that you guys have built a phone relationship for the last couple of months and now you must build one in person. You don't need to worry. It sounds like he's excited about seeing you."

"I know, I know, but it's been awhile since I've been out. I'm a little nervous about running into Gerard and Cheryl or some of his frat bros. You know what I mean?"

"I know exactly how you feel, but I think it will be impossible to avoid Gerard forever. In fact, that will be your final test. Right now, you're okay because, out of sight out of mind. But, girl, I'm here to tell you, when you finally do see him you will feel your heart drop slightly. Just do me a favor and keep your head up no matter what, all right?"

"Yes, of course. I better be going. Ray will be here in forty-five minutes and I need to touch up a little. I'll call you while he's at his cousin's and give you the lowdown."

"Okay babe. Have a good time and don't worry."

Georgette couldn't help the jittery feeling. What if she wasn't attracted to him, after all? What if he wasn't still attracted to her? Oh, she thought, he's not a blind date for goodness' sake. After all, she did spend a considerable amount of time with him at the summit. She hated the way she self-sabotaged everything since she left Gerard. She was sure it had something to do with the fact that she had never lost anything to Cheryl since their high school days. Now it appeared that Cheryl had finally won a battle by winning Gerard over. Not to worry, she promised silently. She vowed to have a fun weekend no matter what. Glancing around the apartment once more, she grabbed her coat, keys, and purse and headed to the train station.

"I can't wait till daylight savings time is over," she said aloud. She despised leaving the house at dark and arriving at home in the dark. It's no wonder crime increased during the daylight savings months. Just two more weeks before she could spring her clock forward again.

Once inside the station, she noticed how crowded it was. How would she find him, anyway? She walked over to the board above and looked for the arrival information. Amtrak number sixty-seven from New York had arrived.

"Whew!" she exclaimed aloud. She could feel the sweat beading on her forehead. "I hate this," she murmured, walking over to the Amtrak station desk to ask for help. She patted her forehead with her silk scarf. She would be glad when this was over. The wait, the anticipation, was killing her. How would she be able to enjoy dinner on a nervous stomach? How could she control her breathing before she saw Ray? Just as she began her breathing exercise, she glanced at the tall figure standing in front of her. The back of him, broad up top but narrowing toward the bottom, faced her. "Oh my gosh," she heard herself utter.

He had on a designer, olive green, long wool trench coat which resembled the dusters from one of those wild, Wild West cowboy movies. His pose was strong, confident. The back of his hairline was perfectly even. God, if he looked as good in front as from behind, she was going to scream. She stood there for what seemed like an eternity until she got up enough courage to tap him on the back. Her heart was doing the flip-flop song as he turned around slowly to greet her. He had a bouquet of white roses surrounded by baby's breath. They looked like he had caught them at a wedding.

"Hi, gorgeous," he bellowed, bowing down to kiss her on the cheek. "How's the queen doing this evening?" he said, placing his arms around her slender back.

"Hi Ray," she whispered in her most seductive voice. "The roses are beautiful, thank you," she said, reaching on her toes to plant a kiss on his lips.

"Anything for my Nubian queen," he said, smiling as he picked up his bag.

"How was the train ride down?"

"It was pleasant. The leg room was sufficient. When I felt a little uncomfortable, I just focused on the prize awaiting me at the end of the tunnel."

Grabbing his hand, she grinned and said, "It's so good to see you in person. I was beginning to think that you were content just talking to me on the phone."

"There is no way I would ever be content having just a phone conversation with you. Don't you ever worry about that."

Georgette blushed. "I made reservations for eight-thirty. We still have an hour and a

half or so. Do you want to drop by your
cousin's house for a minute?"

"Will we have enough time? Will my stuff
be okay in your car?" he asked.

"Tell you what, we could either drop your
bag off at your cousin's place or take it to
my place and get it later on."

"Let's make it easy on you, so this way you
won't have to drive back and forth all night.
I wouldn't want you out too late at night
chauffeuring me around town. Let's just
swing by my cousin's apartment real quick.
This way you can meet her if she's in. How's
that sound?" When Georgette nodded he
said, "She lives at 2334 Jackson Street, apartment U. It's off Broadway and Memorial Ex-
pressway. Do you know where that is?" he
asked.

"As a matter of fact, it's near where we
are going," she said, opening the Honda's
trunk.

"I see we are going to have to have another
talk about buying American-made cars," he
laughed.

"Yeah, yeah, I know we had this conversation before. If you can show me an American
car that's well built and made to last as long
or keep the value as long as a Japanese car,
then I'm sold."

Wait till he sees my stereo and TV equipment, she chuckled to herself, pulling off

into traffic. This is going to be a great weekend, she heard herself say for the tenth time.

"Gerard, pass me that bowl please," Cheryl
said, stirring the pan's contents with a
wooden spoon. She was making stir-fried
vegetables for their evening meal.

"So, what kind of meat are we having with
this mush?" Gerard asked, knitting his brow.

"I thought we would have a wholesome
vegetarian meal. It's a new recipe I got from
one of the guys at work."

"Wholesome? What the heck is a wholesome meal without some red, juicy, artery-
clogging, cholesterol-building meat? Is this
all we are having, for real?" he asked.

"Yes, Gerard," Cheryl said with a heavy
sigh. "And some feta cheese bread."

"Feta *what*? What is that, some kind of deli
food for rats? Girl, if I had known that all I
was getting for dinner was some Weight
Watchers cuisine, I would have eaten before
I got here," Gerard huffed, walking out of
the kitchen.

"You are so ungrateful sometimes, Gerard.
Did it ever occur to you that I spent a lot of
time and money to make this dish just right?"
she asked angrily.

"You couldn't have sprung for some shrimp
to go with that cow grass?" he yelled back at
her, turning on the Bulls versus Pistons game.

"You mean alfalfa sprouts, don't you? Dinner will be served in a few minutes. You might want to wash your hands before you get too involved in that game. I don't know what you men see in all them dudes running up and down the court."

"Ssh, Cheryl, I can't hear!" he shouted.

Cheryl continued buzzing around the kitchen, setting the table, pouring the wine, and fixing the plates. She lit the candles that stood in the brass holders. Gerard never offered to assist. He was too busy advising the Bulls' coach on his "retarded calls." After several requests, Gerard reluctantly got up from the living room sofa and affixed himself to the dining room table. He couldn't see the game well from the dining area. He always hated her apartment. It was too small, too congested with knickknacks, plants and books. The stereo equipment was dated and the TV, a temporary remote control version thanks to the local cable company. This girl needed a major makeover from a home designer, he thought as he took a bite of his dinner.

"What the Sam Hill is this?" he asked.

"It's eggplant, Gerard. Quit tripping and eat." Just at that moment, Cheryl felt another wave of nausea. She leaped up from the table and darted into the bathroom. The gurgling and retching behind the bathroom door was too much for Gerard to bear. He quickly followed behind her.

"What's wrong, Cheryl? You all right?"

"Yes, I—I'm fine. I'll be out in a second. It must be all that cow grass," she said, chuckling faintly.

"Darn, and I was just getting into that nutritional, delicious meal. Oh well, there goes my appetite." He laughed.

"Sorry about that, Gerard," she whimpered, walking back down the hallway from the bathroom.

"I guess you shouldn't be eating that horse food," he said, continuing to laugh. "So, what's wrong with you? Are you pregnant or something?"

"Oh God," she heard herself say. Why did he have to ask her that? "Gerard, I don't know. I've been taking my pills like usual, but I've been feeling a little sick these last few days. I hope not . . . but if I was? Then what?"

"What do you mean, then what? You know how I feel about babies. I can't have any right now," he screeched. "And I don't welcome any right now either."

"What are you saying? If I'm pregnant, you wouldn't want me to have it?"

"Hell, no! Furthermore, how can I be sure it's mine, anyway?"

"*What* did you say? What kind of mess is

this? You think the child isn't yours?" she shouted, heading back to the bathroom.

"Why don't you get a test first, so we can have this disagreement later?" he said, returning to the game.

She slammed the bathroom door hard, rattling the medicine chest. Hovering over the toilet, she marveled at how she got involved with such an insensitive, arrogant buzzard.

God, she hoped and prayed she wasn't pregnant. Hearing Gerard yelling from the living room, she cracked the bathroom door slightly. "What did you say Gerard?"

"I said someone is at your door! Do you want me to get it?"

"If you wouldn't mind. It's probably my cousin Ray. I'll be right out."

Georgette, standing behind Ray, didn't see the person who answered the door right away. But she heard the voice. She couldn't mistake the voice.

"How you doing man?" Ray said, shaking Gerard's hand. Georgette's body was still invisible to the host.

"You must be Cheryl's cousin," Gerard replied, turning his back on Ray. "Come on in. She's a little preoccupied at the moment, but she will be right out," he said, once again turning back to the game.

Georgette followed close behind Ray through the doorway until she reached the entrance. Just at that moment, Ray pulled

Georgette to his side. "I'd like you to meet my friend Georgette Willis," Ray said.

Gerard jolted around like a dog chasing its tail, his pupils widening with each heartbeat.

Georgette clinched Ray's arm tighter and tighter as she fought to maintain her composure. Ray immediately sensed the tension. "You two know each other?" he asked. But no one moved or spoke. Georgette's eyes swiftly perused the room. Had she heard correctly, she thought. Cheryl's cousin? Suddenly she heard the voice.

"Is that my favorite cousin's voice I—" Cheryl began to ask, turning the corner. But her sentence was choked off as she glimpsed the other body standing upright in her living room. Cheryl examined the figure for a long moment.

"Hey cuz, what's up, girl? Come give me a hug or something," Ray said, opening his arms as he walked toward Cheryl.

Cheryl didn't move. She was paralyzed by her thoughts and the figure posed in her living room. Finally, she cut her eyes at Ray and blurted, "Ray, what is this, some kind of joke? What's this bitch doing standing in my living room?"

"What do you mean? This is my friend Georgette. She's the person I really came to see," Ray answered with a puzzled look.

"I know who she is! I don't believe this.

Just get her out of my house right now!"
Cheryl commanded.

"Hold on a minute, cuz. What's going
on?" Ray asked.

Gerard, frozen by Georgette's appearance,
never moved his eyes from her. He was too
busy concentrating on her coat, the one he
had purchased for her two Christmases ago.
"Damn!" he mumbled.

"Time out! Somebody want to tell me
what's going on?" Ray pleaded.

"Let's go, Ray," Georgette begged. She
wanted desperately to crawl under the near-
est rock. *God, please,* she prayed quietly, *let
this nightmare end right now.*

"Why? What's the problem here?" Ray demanded.

"There won't be a problem if you get that
witch out of my damn house right this minute!" Cheryl said. "No, better yet, I'll do it
myself!" With that, Cheryl charged at Georgette.

"Now hold on one damn minute," Ray
said, but it was too late.

Cheryl swung at Georgette with all her
might, barely missing her cheek. Georgette,
dodging the swing to the best of her ability,
defensively fired up her right hand and
slapped Cheryl across the face. She gasped
at the impact of the blow. Just as Georgette
tried to back away, Gerard jumped between
them, with intentions of breaking them up.

But his restraint of Georgette caused her to fall back against the table.

"Yo man, what the hell is wrong with you, pushing her like that?" Ray said, shoving Gerard's chest.

"Look, brother, your best bet is to stay out of it and out of my face!" Gerard said, standing toe to toe with Ray. It didn't matter that this brother was some five inches taller than he. He was mad and ready to kick somebody's ass if he had to. The tension was dangerously thick.

"I'll kill you, I swear I will!" Cheryl screamed at the top of her lungs.

"Kill *me?* What did I ever do to you?" Georgette said angrily.

"Would the both of you please just shut up!" Ray ordered, pulling Georgette past Cheryl to the front door. "Get your purse and let's go," he said.

In an effort to push Georgette out of the house, Cheryl tripped over a chair leg and fell onto the floor. Cheryl hit the floor with a heavy thump upon her descent. The howl following the fall silenced everyone.

"Lynn! Are you okay?" Ray kneeled down beside his cousin, and proceeded to help her up. But she couldn't get up. The wind had been knocked out of her.

Gerard stood over Cheryl looking perplexed. What was happening here? First, the crazy stuff with Georgette and now this. "Are you all right Cheryl?" Gerard asked.

"No," she answered faintly. "I think I'm miscarrying. Maybe I should go to the hospital."

"Miscarrying? You're pregnant? Do you want me to take you to the hospital Lynn?" Ray asked.

"No! Ray, just get that woman out of my house."

Ray and Gerard turned to face Georgette. Ray walked over to Georgette, pulled her gently toward his chest and said, "Come on, let's go."

"She's pregnant, Ray, can you believe it?" Georgette said, somewhat dazed. "He told me he never wanted kids. How could he do this?" she said.

Cheryl looked at Gerard then shook her head. "God save me from myself for I don't know what I'm doing," she murmured staggering to the sofa, "Ray, just get her out of here."

"Okay Lynn, I'll call you later to see how you're doing," Ray promised.

"Lynn?" Gerard repeated, raising his eyebrows.

"Let's go, Georgette. Are you going to be all right?" Ray asked. He didn't wait for an answer; he was too tired to even care. He picked up his bag in one hand, put his other hand around Georgette's shoulder, and headed out the door.

Georgette and Ray sat in the car awhile until she calmed down. She was deeply disturbed by the news about Cheryl's pregnancy. Ray gazed out the window until the rage seeped away. He offered to drive as she cranked the engine, but she refused, assuring him that everything was okay. "Everything will be okay Ray, it just has to be," she prayed, pulling into traffic.

Fifteen

After dropping Cheryl off, Gerard decided to swing by his brother's house and have a heart-to-heart. All the action with Cheryl, the emergency room, the baby, Georgette, and her new man was too much for him to handle. Dwight would know exactly what to say to help overcome his depression. "A baby? Why now, Lord?" he asked aloud. He was feeling betrayed by Cheryl. How could she let this happen? She must have known what she was doing. He shut the engine off; 12:30 A.M. was displayed on the beemer's clock. Deciding to risk waking up Beverly and the kids, he timidly pressed the bell. It seemed like eons before the hall lights came on.

"Who is it?" bellowed the voice behind the oak door.

"It's me. Gerard. Open the door."

"Hey man, what's wrong? Something happen to Ma?" Dwight asked.

"Naw man, nothing like that. I just need to talk to you, that's all. I know it's late and all but I had to go somewhere." His face looked scuffed like a pair of old shoes. His hair was untamed and it looked like he had been sleeping in his clothes. His shirt was wrinkled and hanging out of the back of his pants.

"Come on in. What's wrong, G? You look like you haven't slept in God knows how long." Dwight closed the door behind him. He motioned to Gerard to head through the large marble foyer toward the huge family room. Gerard could tell that a fire had been burning in the brick fireplace earlier that night. The room was airy with nineteen-foot ceilings and two skylights. The four-bedroom, four-bathroom house was an architectural masterpiece with unique angles and cabinet designs throughout. His brother had done well, he thought, plopping down on the black leather sofa. He could hear his sister-in-law moving around upstairs.

"Honey what's wrong?" Beverly asked, peeping over the loft.

"It's Gerard, baby. Everything is okay. You can go back to bed."

"Gerard? Is he all right?"

"Hey Beverly, sorry for waking you," Gerard called up to her. "I need to speak to Dwight about some things, that's all."

"Well, don't be such a stranger, Gerard.

Your niece and nephew would like to see your face sometime in the near future."

Gerard gave a weak laugh. He felt guilty about not spending enough time with Jasmine and Joshua.

"So, what's up, little brother? It's unlike you to come by at this time of the night," Dwight asked after Beverly went back into the bedroom.

"I can't begin to tell you about the night from hell I had. First of all I should probably tell you that you'll soon be an uncle." Dwight was silent as he leaned back against the recliner.

"An uncle? Who's pregnant?"

Gerard took a deep breath. "Cheryl."

"Cheryl? How? Why? I mean, I know how but why her of all people?" Dwight emphasized. There was a stretch of silence before Gerard began summarizing the evening's phenomenon. He told Dwight about the fight between Georgette and Cheryl as well as his own altercation with Cheryl's cousin Ray. He revealed his feelings about seeing Georgette with Ray and about Cheryl's pregnancy.

"So what are you going to do, Gerard?"

"I wish I knew. All I can tell you for sure is that I do not want any children especially out of wedlock. It will kill Mama if she knew I had a child without having a wife first. You know how she is."

"Never mind what it would do to Mama.

Mama is living her life and you have got to continue living yours. Who's to say how she would really feel? Anyway, that's beside the point. The issue at hand is whether you will support that girl and the baby."

"It's obvious you don't like her very much." Gerard hung his head. "Of course I will pay child support and all that stuff. The fact is, I don't want this baby."

"How far along is she?"

"The doctor said it looks like seven weeks or so. They won't be sure till she sees her doc and gets all the dates figured out."

"Well I'm glad to hear that you will be responsible. I'm sure Dad is smiling down on you right now. How you feeling about your other situation?"

"What, about Georgette? Whew! I don't know. I'm not going to lie, it kind of hurt me to see her with another brother. She was looking gorgeous as usual. I still can't believe it! Out of all the brothers in the world she found one that's related to Cheryl. Who would have figured?"

"Gerard, I know this is not the time but you really need to evaluate your feelings about Georgette, you know? She's a wonderful sister and very supportive of you and your career goals. I was hoping you two could have worked out something."

"Yeah, I know. Mama said the same thing to me several times. I think this time it's too late. Too much has happened between us. Plus she's got a new sugar daddy."

"So what? You two have a history. And a mighty lengthy one. You know you two belong together. The only thing I can tell you is you've got to be strong, stay away from temptation, and ask the Man upstairs to keep you every day. When that doesn't seem to work then ask yourself, is it worth losing everyone and everything I love?"

"I appreciate that Dwight, but it gets so hard sometimes. I get the panties thrown at me all day and all night long. What's a brother to do?" Gerard grinned slightly. "Anyway, Georgette would never forgive me now. Hell, with Cheryl being pregnant? I don't think so."

"You never know unless you try," Dwight encouraged.

"No. I told her I never wanted kids, with her or anybody. And now Cheryl's pregnant."

"Damn, G, you sure have a lot to overcome. I tell you what, if you need me I'm here. But if you need some real guidance and conscious relief, He's up there. Bow down tonight and pray like your life depended on it because you will need all the strength you can to overcome this one. Oh, and before I forget, stay away from that mind-altering stimulus, you understand me? Now grab some sofa and get some z's. We'll talk some more tomorrow over Beverly's apple pancakes."

"Thanks, Dwight," Gerard said, laying back on the sofa.

"I love you, man. You're my only brother, so take it easy on yourself. See you in the A.M." Dwight smiled and walked away.

Flipping back and forth on the sofa for several minutes, Gerard rolled over and got down on his knees. Upon completion of the Lord's Prayer, the only prayer he'd said in four years, he could feel the tears swelling up in his eyes. "Lord, please help me!" he moaned. Precisely at that moment, he could feel a great load being lifted off his chest. He glanced around the room seeking the person that he felt was in the room with him. Feeling overtaken by tears, he wept for a while longer and then sprang up and smiled. "Oh my God!" he responded in a joyous manner, he was experiencing an epiphany. It came and left as quick as a bolt of lighting. But Gerard Jenkins now knew what he had to do.

Georgette needed a hot bath to calm herself. What Ray needed was an interpretation of the evening's events. Resisting the urge to pressure Georgette for an explanation during the drive home, he would attempt to begin the interrogation. Following her to the bathroom, he stopped in the doorway. As Georgette turned the knobs to the faucet, a rush of water gushed out. Sitting on the edge of the tub, she struggled to pull off her boots. Ray immediately came to her aid. She held on to the corner of the tub while he wiggled the boots free. She turned around till her back faced him and pointed to the zipper to her blouse. He responded by sliding the zipper down until her turquoise camisole was fully exposed. She unbuttoned her skirt and pulled it down until the matching turquoise silk thongs were showing. Ray didn't budge. He wasn't uncomfortable with Georgette's display of openness.

"Why don't you get comfortable too?" she said, adding some bubble beads to the steady stream of water.

Ray obliged by taking off his shirt, then his sleeveless T-shirt. Georgette couldn't help but stare at the curly hair covering his defined chest. His biceps were bulging and his chest displayed well-developed muscles.

"So, do you want to tell me what this stuff with you and my cousin is all about?" he asked, untying his shoes.

"Ray, I know you must be thinking the worst about me right now, but I really don't know how or where to begin," Georgette said, shutting off the bathwater.

"Just start from the beginning or wherever it might make sense to me," Ray replied, lowering the toilet seat lid. "Do you mind if I sit here while we talk?"

"Not at all," she frailly mumbled. Ray stepped out of the bathroom so she could strip off her undergarments and plop into the tub of bubbles. After she sunk beneath the bubbles, Ray re-entered and sat on the seat.

"There is so much to tell. I guess I'll give you a brief summary of my history with your cousin. Are you sure you want to hear all the details?"

"I'm sure," he said kneeling beside the tub.

"Would you care to join me?" Georgette shyly asked. "It's been a long day for you, too."

He smiled. "Are you sure?"

"Please do," she sighed.

Georgette averted her eyes as Ray undressed and stepped in the tub. He grabbed the washcloth, and began making small circles on her back. He noticed the tension dissipating. She launched the story of her and her long-time rival. Before long, Ray's entire body was surrounded by bubbles. He continued massaging Georgette's shoulder and neck until she was totally limber. She proceeded with her narrative leaving no stone unturned. Ray silently absorbed the information while occasionally dripping her back with the washcloth. *What am I supposed to do now?* he thought He knew he was in love with Georgette the first moment he laid eyes on her. But he also loved Cheryl Lynn. After all, she was family.

Rising from the water, Ray examined Georgette's body once again. She had the most curves he'd ever seen on a woman. Straining to keep control of his nature, he found an excuse to linger in the water a little longer.

"I'm so tired, Ray," she said, drying off and wrapping the towel around her shapely form. "I feel like I'm walking in a daze and everything is a blur. Can we finish the conversation in the morning?"

"Sure, that's fine," he agreed.

Georgette headed toward the paisley comforter and pillow shams. She dropped the towel and fell into the sheets. Lying facedown, exposing her entire backside, she began to drift to sleep. Ray stood in the doorway adoring the view. Perhaps it was the soft curve lines or the figurine-like pose that mesmerized him so. All he knew was that he wanted her, it nearly broke his control by bathing with her. Even now after all the chaos of the evening, Ray still revered Georgette. The problem now facing him seemed more intense, like trying to gather all your tax papers at 11:59 P.M. on the fifteenth of April. The dilemma, where, oh, where should he sleep?

Trespassing on Georgette's precious personal space, Ray eased into bed cupping her waist. She automatically slid her back closer to him. He placed a soft kiss on her warm back. She moaned pleasurably.

"Ray," she turned to face him. He was struck again by how lovely she was. "I'm not really ready for the intimate thing yet. So much has happened to me over the last few months, you know?"

"I understand, Georgette. I'll be a gentleman," he laughed.

She held his hand. "Good," she said with a brilliant smile. "I feel comfortable and secure cuddled up with you. Are you sure that won't cause a problem for you?"

"Not if you don't keep squirming the way you are." He kissed her on the back of her neck and drew her tighter. Clutching his right hand, she raised it to her lips and kissed it. "Good night, Mr. Fuschée."

"Good night, sweetheart."

Lying on a sheet covering the newly shellacked hardwood floors, Cheryl focused on the small night-light plugged in the hallway. The coolness of the floor penetrating the sheet felt refreshing to her. It had been a long, exhausting, heated day. The night color of her apartment exuded tranquility. Through all the pitch silence, she could still discern the "clink" of the ice separating in the cold glass of water. What did it mean to be pregnant? she pondered.

Basically it meant to grow up, settle down, be responsible, be reasonable, be rational, be sensible, be sensitive. How could she be any of those things in anyone's eyes now? Her cousin was obviously smitten with her arch rival. Her so-called man made it painfully aware that fatherhood and his name didn't belong in the same sentence together. Her fellow sorors would swear she got pregnant on purpose. Why was this happening to her? The pills never failed her before. She was convinced that this was punishment for all of her nonconforming ways.

She would name the baby after Gerard if it were a boy. She couldn't decide what to name the child if it were a girl. Moving out of her one-bedroom apartment would be a must once the baby was born. Maybe Gerard would change his mind and marry her after all. He seemed like the type of brother who would want to give his child a legitimate name and home. But she saw how Gerard looked at Georgette tonight. She would have to make sure that they would never get back together. She smiled to herself as she remembered the errand she ran after Gerard dropped her back at home from the hospital. She'd make sure Gerard would be hers and stay hers.

The next morning, she needed to see

her doctor. Then she needed desperately to cry but not alone. Her parents would be back from their yearly trip to the Bahamas tomorrow so she would be propped on their sofa by late afternoon awaiting their arrival. They would be disappointed but supportive. Her folks weren't the meddling type always coming over unannounced, calling any hour of the Godforsaken night, prying, spying, preaching the same things over and over. The Grays were experts when it came to sticking to their business at hand. Her dad would want to have a little chat with Gerard just to be safe but she won't allow it. No sir, she thought. She would handle the ordeal for once in her life. It was time to grow up.

Sixteen

"Rise and shine, precious," Ray whispered softly in Georgette's ear.

"What time is it?" she murmured.

"Time to get up," he said, chuckling and shaking her lightly.

It was obvious to Georgette that this brother didn't have a clue that even the most gentle bodily attempts to awaken her were fighting gestures. *Well*, she decided, *he'll learn*. "What's that aroma filling up the house? Is that bacon I smell?" she said, suddenly springing up from under the covers.

"Maybe it is, maybe it ain't. But the only way to find out is to get to stepping into the bathroom. Grub will be served in thirty minutes or less."

"Why do I need to go to the bathroom? What, you afraid of a little morning breath?" she snickered wobbling to the bathroom. She's a streaker for sure, Ray thought, as she didn't attempt to cover her nakedness.

"You don't own a robe, I guess," he said, heading back to the kitchen.

"Maybe I do, maybe I don't, but you wouldn't see it this weekend or any weekend for that matter."

"Is that right?" he smiled, raising an eyebrow. "Betcha when that ice cold Chicago winter wind ripples that skin you'll change your tune."

"In that case, none of my robes will be warm enough. I guess I'll have to break down and buy that fur robe unless your heat works as good as it did last night."

"Now Georgette, why you want to go and say something provocative like that? You know good and well that heat, as well as any subject surrounding it, rises."

He heard the bathroom door shut and the shower running and was relieved. This flirtatious stuff had to cease and soon. It was only a matter of time before things got out of control. Despite all the turmoil of the evening before, he was happy. He was delighted to be spending time with Georgette in person.

But he had to see Lynn. He would have Georgette drop him off over at Lynn's later if she felt up to it. Perhaps that would be too much to ask of her. If it were too troublesome, he would catch mass transit or rent a car.

"It's chow time, so light a fire under them there feet," he yelled through the bathroom door. He hoped she would have some clothes on this time so he wouldn't have to continue to test his strength. No such luck, he thought, turning to face wet, dripping, honeysuckle-colored flesh. "Georgette, please tell me I'm not going to have to break bread with you acting like Lady Godiva. I don't think I could concentrate on my food," he said, looking down at the floor. He could feel himself blushing.

Georgette laughed as she strategically covered herself with her hands. "You crack me up, Ray. Standing there hanging your head like a schoolboy. Of course I will put some clothes on. All the towels were sour from lying on the floor last night so I had to dash out here to get one. I apologize for making you feel uncomfortable. I guess I feel a little bit too free around you. I'll be in the kitchen in a second okay?"

"Take as long as you need, just make sure you come out here with something more on than patches of hair." They both giggled realizing that she had been a bit of an exhibitionist the last twenty-four hours.

When Georgette returned wearing jeans and a baggy shirt, they sat at the table. Ray decided to broach the question. "I'm thinking about going over to Lynn's later to see how she's doing. Do you think you could drop me off?" There was a moment of silence and gloom hovering over the table. "How are you feeling about that?"

"How am I supposed to feel? I mean, she is your cousin and all. I suppose I have no choice but to take you over there."

"Thanks Georgette, I know it's still a tender spot with you. I don't want to hurt you any more than you already have been."

"I'll be fine Ray, really. What time are we talking about?"

"In a few hours, I guess. Did you have something special planned for us today?"

"Not really. I figure we would do some shopping then try and catch the 76ers this evening."

"The who? Sixers? Who are they?" he teased.

"Okay, so Chicago has a fairly decent team, but you can't appreciate viewing another professional team in person?" she asked with a tilt of her head.

"If I must," he exasperated. She gave him one of her crooked smiles. He returned the gesture just as the doorbell's chime sounded. "Who could that be?" she wondered aloud, heading to the door. Ray's posture stiffened somewhat, grimacing at the idea that it was the return of the nightmare on Phillips Street. He heard her thanking someone as he rose to accompany her in the living room.

"An overnight delivery," she uttered, returning to the table.

"I wonder what it is, I wasn't expecting anything," she stated while opening the package.

"I can't believe this! That girl is still tripping!" she said, handing the package to Ray. "See what I mean? I'm sorry she's your cousin and all but she is one deranged woman!" Ray stared at the picture of her cousin and Georgette's old flame. He shook his head, looked up at the ceiling and returned to the picture.

The photograph was of Lynn and Gerard kissing intimately at some gala affair. Sitting at the table clasping the picture, he gazed at Georgette. Out of all the women in the world, why did he have to fall in love with someone his favorite cousin hated? He didn't speak, he just laid the picture on the table and leaned back in the chair with his hands behind his head, a posture he adopted when he was trying to filter through situations. He had no idea Lynn disliked Georgette that much. Why would Lynn go to such an extent to inflict pain on anyone?

Ray shook his head in dismay. "Georgette, I don't know what to say to you. I feel partly responsible for Lynn's actions."

"Ha! Don't take responsibility for her. This has been my battle—hers and mine—for a long time. It's unfortunate that the enemy I'm fighting is one of your favorite cousins. Where exactly does that leave you?"

"Hell, I don't know. I suppose I need to hear her side in all this. I think I should go over there and have a little talk with her." He stretched from the oak folding chair and headed toward the phone. He was going to get to the bottom of this nonsense if it required his last bit of breath.

"Boy those pancakes were smoking, Sis. I'll have to come over more often," teased Gerard.

"Whatever it takes to see your little face more often. I know the kids enjoyed your visit. Right kids?" Beverly asked.

"Yeah!!" screamed the twins in unison.

"Get your things and let's go. We need to meet your grandpa in forty-five minutes. See you later honey." Beverly gave Dwight a quick smack on the lips, hugged Gerard, grabbed her duffel bag, and beckoned the kids once more. "I'll call you when I get to Daddy's. There's leftover meat loaf and mashed potatoes in the fridge. You take care, Gerard, till I see you again." She was out the door and in the Volvo and down the street by the time Gerard got to his car.

Dwight, accompanying him to the beemer, gave him the brother-to-brother handshake. "Are you planning to talk to Cheryl today?"

"Yeah, probably. I feel somewhat obligated to check in and see how she's doing. Do you think it would be wrong of me to marry her for the sake of the kid?"

Dwight nearly choked at Gerard's statement. "Marry her?" Dwight tried to restrain his disapproval. "Have you wrapped up your feelings regarding Georgette? Remember how much Georgette meant to you. I don't know how deeply in love with Cheryl you are . . ."

"I'm not in love with Cheryl. I just have a responsibility to her and the baby."

"Well, I'm not talking about love," his brother continued. "Who do you want to spend the rest of your life with? Who makes you happy? Who fulfills you and supports you? To me, it sounds like only one person."

Gerard was quiet as he mulled over his brother's words. Visions of Georgette's lovely face filled his mind. He remembered her laugh, her insightfulness, her grace. He adored her insightfulness, her creativity, her goals. He loved the way she made him feel special, brilliant, and sexy. Cheryl never made him feel the way Georgette made him feel. No woman could replace her, which is why he always returned to her, time and time again. She was the object of his love and desire. How could he be so foolish as to want Cheryl over Georgette?

"I did finally address the fact that I still love Georgette very much and that this whole breakup was unnecessary. I have no one to blame but myself. Had I been on the up and up in the first place, none of this would have happened. Anyway, I'm responsible for a little life now and I've got to start thinking about someone other than myself for a change."

Dwight could not believe what he was hearing. "I guess you must have had a pretty long session with the Main Man last night, huh? Well, that's a good thing. All I will say is follow your heart. The heart, if you listen closely, will point you in the right direction. Keep me posted, okay?"

Seventeen

Having dropped Ray off, Georgette was happy to be back at home. She snatched the picture of Gerard and Cheryl off the kitchen table. The more she stared at the picture, the more she was able to justify her behavior of the previous night. She sat at the table examining the photo like an expert witness would do in a trial. The way she was feeling about everything, there might well be a murder trial if things didn't settle down soon. She couldn't help but feel consumed with anger and pain.

The nerve of Cheryl, trapping Gerard with a baby just to ensure she'd have a place in his life. But who was she kidding? Gerard was just as much to blame, though, running around in this day and age having unprotected sex.

She wanted to call Melinda and give her the scoop, but she didn't want to subject her friend to another one of her dramatic scenes. She would wait till the weekend was over and then call. Melinda would probably threaten to drive down and kick Cheryl's butt. Was it just her, or did it seem like no one really cared for Cheryl?

Pouring the freshly squeezed orange juice into a glass, Cheryl handed it to Ray.

"Ray, you know I can talk to you about anything, but right now I don't feel much like reviewing my and Georgette's history. I can't believe I even uttered her name. Look, I'm all right, okay? Besides, it's obvious you have a thing for her."

"Lynn, that's another issue. Right now I am concerned about your well-being. Tell me about the father of this baby. Do you love him, or what's up?"

Cheryl frowned. "What difference does it make now? I'm pregnant, and that's that."

"How do you feel about possibly raising a child alone? Is he planning to acknowledge the baby, or you, for that matter?"

"Ray, what's with all the questions, really? This ordeal is tough enough without my very own cousin siding with my arch foe."

Ray didn't bother to respond. He knew it would come down to this. Georgette must be feeling the same way. She didn't say two words to him the entire trip over here. She didn't even bother to turn around and wave goodbye. She just gunned that little Honda of hers and sped off down the road. He didn't fault her, though. It was a difficult situation for them both.

"Got any Maalox or anything?" he asked.

"I think so. Why, what's wrong with you?"

"Seems like my ulcer is about to go bozonkers again. Listen, when and if you want to talk about things, you need to know that I will always be here. Regardless of this mess we've gotten into, you are still my favorite cousin and I love you, you understand that?"

Cheryl gave him a grateful hug. God, at least there was someone on this planet that loved her. "Mom and Dad will be back in a few hours. I was thinking about heading over there and sharing the news with them. You want to come with me for some moral support? Besides, you know if you left Philly without seeing your auntie she would never forgive you. So how's about it?"

"Sure, Lynn, count me in. Are you sure you want to let the cat out of the bag so soon though? Wouldn't it be better to wait awhile, I mean, till you know what's up with you and what's-his-name?" he asked.

"Gerard. And maybe you're right. It probably is too soon to involve the folks."

The sudden thumping at the door made Cheryl jump. "Who could that be?" she said, raising her left brow.

Shrugging his shoulders, Ray replied, "Beats me, but I hope we're not in for a repeat of last night's event."

The pounding erupted again. Looking back at Ray, she hesitantly tiptoed over to the door and glanced through the peephole. She then lowered her head, backing away slowly. "It's Gerard," she whispered.

Ray eased himself down on the worn sofa. "Don't bother to answer it," he advised.

"I don't plan on it," she said, backing away from the door.

Gerard, deciding that Cheryl probably needed a day in bed after the events of the previous night, headed back to the streets. He wanted to talk to her and try to assess her feelings regarding the birth of the baby. He wanted her to know that he would support her in raising the child. This situation was certainly going to be a test of endurance for him.

Pulling onto the highway, Gerard thought to make another attempt at salvation. He lifted the car phone from its cradle and entered 02. The digits began the automation process, which was abruptly choked off by Gerard's pressing of the reset button. "No," he reckoned aloud, he would resolve the other matter in person. Exiting off the highway onto a residential street, he pulled over to the curb. He was sure that stopping by Georgette's unannounced would only precipitate another scene. "Patience, patience, patience!"

he repeated several times until the anxiety
subsided. How long was this Ray character going to be in town anyway? Furthermore, when
and where did Georgette meet him? It was
obvious that this brother would have defended
her to his death. Maybe their relationship was
more serious than he'd imagined last night.
She was moving on without him.

He laid his head on the headrest and
tuned in to the sounds and sights of the city
streets. Where would he raise a child nowadays? Certainly not in the 'hood. Not if he
could help it. Well, he wouldn't have to
worry about that so long as he kept perform-
ing at EPI Corporation. If he closed the deal
in Chicago in the next month or so, he would
be set. The company had plans to offer him
a partnership if he pulled off the multimil-
lion dollar deal. He figured his yearly salary
would boost from $85,000 a year to $140,000
plus bonuses. He would postpone law school
indefinitely if the Chicago deal worked out.
He didn't know many young lawyers who
could boast about raking in that kind of cash.
The first thing he would do, would be to set
up a trust fund for the baby. Then, he would
purchase a house or a multidwelling unit
somewhere in Philly and renovate it. He
could lease it out to ensure a consistent
monthly income. He would use that income
to help supplement anything Cheryl needed
for the baby along with any child support

payments. That would mean he would have to amend his Will a little. His mom had been his main beneficiary, with Dwight and the twins receiving equal shares of one of his several policies.

He would leave the house on Martha's Vineyard to Georgette. She loved the house so much, and it might make up for all the things she had had to endure with him. He wanted to thank her for being there for him at his father's death, for the many term papers she had edited. Not to mention make up for the pain of dealing with the other women. He wasn't sure to what extent Georgette knew about the others, but she certainly knew about Cheryl. That was more than enough for her to bear.

The intermittent flash of red light reflected in his rearview mirror snapped him out of his reverie. He heard a bullhorn switch on and a husky voice immediately bellowed, "Everything okay, sir?" The cop approached the car.

Gerard, accustomed to how trigger-happy cops were with regard to black males, slowly let down the window. "Yeah, officer, everything's fine. I was feeling a little sleepy, so I pulled over to catch a quick nap." That should do it, he reasoned.

"Okay, son, but you should probably try and make it to a hotel or something. It's not good to hang out on the shoulder for too long." The officer gave him a skeptical glare as he passed, perusing the beemer's interior. Gerard hated the way white officers referred to black men as "son," no matter how old they looked. Reflecting on the many drives he had taken on the New Jersey Turnpike with his dad, he recalled one incident when one of the troopers had flagged them over. His dad, whose hair at the time was a distinguished gray, had said to Gerard, "It's going to be okay. I'm sure I wasn't speeding." It wasn't the way that the trooper had approached the car, his magnum drawn, that Gerard remembered so vividly. It wasn't even the officer's remark about his dad's brand new Lincoln Continental. It was the officer's reference to his dad as "son" that stuck out in his mind. Seemed like from that day on, Gerard had a hard time tolerating the word used in that context. Gerard took a deep breath and merged into the evening's light traffic. Unable to accomplish his mission, he decided to head home. He knew in time that everything would be all right. He saw the vision and he believed in it.

Georgette finally got in touch with Melinda. After sharing the Cheryl story with her friend, she laid down in the middle of the living room floor. She put the CD player on random selection so that she could receive small doses of Luther Vandross, Stevie Wonder, and Phyllis Hyman. Melinda was right, her life was becoming like one of those afternoon soap operas. With her hands behind her head, knees bent, she stared at the ceiling and got lost in her thoughts.

She hadn't done this in a long time, laying in the dark with just the small light radiating from the stereo, being comforted by the music. Laying here all night wouldn't be a problem, especially with six CDs flipping randomly. As tempting as it was to remain right where she was, she knew she would have to get up sooner or later. Ray had promised to come back sometime this evening.

She wondered what Gerard was thinking at this very moment. Not that it made a whole heck of a lot of difference what homey was up to, she thought. This entire mess was his fault, anyway. How dare he drag her down to his level. And what about Ray, what was she supposed to do about him now? The fork in the road had become more like a pair of freshly sharpened scissors. To hang in there with Ray equated to pain because of his close relation with Cheryl. Yet to imagine, even for a brief second, a reunion with Gerard, was ludicrous. Let the truth be known, she wasn't sure what she should do. In her heart of hearts she knew she was drawn to Ray.

Ray was like a dream prince brought to

life. Strong, handsome, sensitive, intelligent, sincere. "He's too good to be true," she marveled. Luther was serenading her now as she glanced up at the Mikasa clock on the wall unit; the little hand was on the seven. Ray said he would call if he couldn't make it. She desperately hoped that he would return tonight. But maybe Cheryl, or Lynn, or whatever her name was had convinced him not to have anything to do with her. "Oh well," she sighed. She knew her limit. With all she'd been through the past year or two with Gerard, maybe it was time to take a break, a sabbatical from the relationship scene. Her mind was as worn out as her heart.

When the phone started ringing, she turned the volume down on the stereo and reached for it. "Hello?" she managed to utter.

"Georgette? Hi, it's Ray. I should be there by nine or so, is that all right with you?"

"That's fine. I'll be here."

"Good. I'm at my aunt's house now, so I'll see you in a few."

It almost made her laugh, the way Ray was so concerned and thoughtful. What a difference between Ray and Gerard. Gerard may or may not have called in advance. If he had called, he certainly wouldn't have asked her permission about an arrival time. He would have taken for granted that she would be home waiting for him and that he would get there when and if he could. All it takes is a little bit of common courtesy and respect, she thought. "That's it!" she declared. Gerard just hadn't respected her. She shook her head, smiling. Where in the world had Ray been all her life?

Gerard, still exhausted from the night before, dropped his bag at the front door. He turned the dimmer to the living room light up as he lifted the receiver to check his messages. The house was damp and cool and the plants needed some water. He had ten messages, none of which meant anything to him. The frat wanted to know if he was planning to attend the Penn Relays the weekend after next; another frat brother wanted to list him as a reference; his cousin in Boston wanted to know if he could rent the house on Martha's Vineyard for July 4th; and Dwight wanted him to call him when he got in. Ten messages and none of them from Cheryl or Georgette. He thought for sure that he would have gotten a message or some kind of reaction from Georgette after she heard about the pregnancy. She was probably too preoccupied with Cheryl's cousin Ray, old chump ass. All this time he thought she was too scared or too embarrassed to show her face, but he guessed wrong. It made him kind of wonder if she had been seeing homeboy all along. How dare she, he thought.

Realizing that he pretty much deserved whatever happened to him, he sprang up from the chair and headed for the bathroom.

Reaching in the top cabinet drawer, he pulled out a small black cloth bag. Dumping the contents on the vanity, he grabbed the small garbage can. One by one, he began dumping the items. First the small mirror, then the small razor blade along with the thin straw. Finally, the small packet of white powder.

After this ritual, he quickly tied up the trash bag and headed for the large Dumpster in the alleyway outside. Hurling the bag toward the Dumpster as if it were a spiraling football, he turned and walked back toward the door. Until a thick body stood directly in his pathway. He could feel the adrenaline starting to kick in once he noticed another figure standing to his right.

"What's up?" he asked the burly man standing before him.

"Yo, brother, could you spare some change?" asked the body to the right of him.

"Maybe, depends on how much you talking?" Gerard knew he had to be cool and not lose his temper. He had heard about people being mugged but he never thought it would happen to him outside his very own home. If he could only get out of the dark

and to the front door. Then he could figure
out from the looks of the brothers what their
intentions were. He knew if he could convince these dudes to let him run inside for
a minute to get some change, things would
be okay. But what if they wanted to follow
him? Naw, there were too many people coming in and out of the apartment building.
He decided to try and win their trust. The
bigger man was closing in on him.

"What you got man? We ain't got all day!"

"Lord, I'm not ready to die, so please help
me out here," Gerard said out loud.

"Who you talking to, chump?" snarled the
brother to the right of him. At first, Gerard
didn't say a thing. He just recited the Lord's
Prayer over and over in his head. The words
became more jumbled as the pace quickened
because of the metal object gleaming at his
head. He thought about Georgette and how
much hurt he'd caused her. He thought
about Cheryl and the baby, his mother, his
brother, his niece and nephew. He would be
ready to die for any of them, but for this? A
random mugging? No way! He had too much
to set straight in his life. He knew that because the Lord had shown him. How ironic,
he thought, to finally dump the narcotics that
could have sent him to an early grave only
to be confronted by death on his return back
to his own house. He calculated how much
money he had inside. It wouldn't be any

good to anyone except these thugs if he were dead. Nothing would be worth a damn if he were dead.

"Listen," he finally said. "I don't have any money on me right now but I may be able to get you some. Are you guys hungry or something?" Damn, that sounded stupid, he thought.

"Hell, yeah, we're hungry, and so are my kids. So how much you got on you, rich boy?" the burly man said, shoving him to the ground.

"Are you sure it's not for drugs or drinks or something?" Where was all this talk coming from, Gerard thought with a look of surprise.

"I told you what it's for. How many times we gonna ask you? Seems like to me you hard of hearing. Deaf as if you had a bullet in the head," the big man continued. The man on the right never said anything.

"Would you brothers trust me to go get you some cash and come right back?"

"What?" laughed the men. "You crazy, boy, you know that? You think we gonna wait here till you go and call the cops?!" The big man raised the metal object with the intention to strike a blow.

Gerard jumped up and grabbed his arm. "Hold it man! I'm serious. If you and your family are hungry and need to eat, let me go get some cash. Okay? If you don't trust me, let him come with me. But first I wanna pat him down to make sure he's not packing."

"Oh, so that he can go upstairs and get his head blown off? Where you from, boy, 'cause you ain't playing the game right. See, we in charge here, not you. You dig?" said the big man.

"I dig, but I don't have any cash on me, okay? Listen, call it what you must. All I know is I just came off such a mental trip, I just tossed away about five hundred dollars worth of cocaine. I'm trying, man, I'm really trying, to turn over a new leaf. So, like I said, if you want some money, lay low here and I will go upstairs and get you some funds. At least you and your kids will have something to eat tonight," Gerard explained.

"What you saying? Just like that you gonna give me some money. How come you waste your money on all that stuff? Can't you sell it back and get your money back?" the big man asked.

"It ain't about that now. I'm changing my ways and now I know what's right. So you guys wait here while I go get you what I have." Gerard eased by the big man. He could feel the sweat dripping from his forehead. He shouldn't have turned his back like he did. Better yet, he shouldn't have agreed to do anything. But he knew in his heart he was being guided by a higher spirit.

"Man, you better not be f'ing with me!" the big man threatened.

"Wait here, but come from out of the alley. Somebody might get hurt. Just sit here on the steps and give me five minutes."

Gerard hopped up the stairs three at a time. Once inside his apartment, he thought about calling the police. In fact, he halfway wished he had a weapon to go and blow them away for scaring him like they had. But instead, he hustled around as fast as he could putting all kinds of food and stuff in plastic bags, steaks, chicken, tuna cans, juice, bread, popcorn, and soup. Then, he went into the bedroom and rummaged through his top drawer till he found a box. Opening it, he grabbed a stack of bills wrapped in a rubber band. From what he could remember, it totaled about five hundred dollars, split between fifties and one-hundred-dollar bills. Glancing around the room to see what else he could give the big man, he noticed his father's Bible sitting on the nightstand. It had been with him all these many nights since his dad's death. It was his shield of protection. He snatched that, too. What the hell was he doing? Everything was moving so fast he didn't have time to think. All he could do was act, follow through, go with the feeling.

Heading back down the stairs with his arms full, he could barely see the two figures through the pane glass doors, they were so scrunched up near the first step. He could tell by the look on their faces that they were surprised. The burly man jumped up and came to his rescue. He grabbed some of the bags from Gerard as he summoned the smaller man to assist. There was a long stare between Gerard and the big man. Gerard knew that the big man was puzzled by the events taking place. Once the two men had the bags evenly distributed, Gerard, holding the Bible in one hand, reached into his pocket with his other hand and said, "Here! This is all I have. I truly hope it will help."

The big man's face softened. He bowed his head down in embarrassment. He was thinking about how he might have snuffed this man out for the dollars in his pocket.

Gerard handed him the large book. "This was my father's Bible. He gave it to me before he died and told me it would be my safety net anytime I felt like I was falling. I want you to have it, big man. I only have the one, so you'll have to share."

"That's my son," the big man said, looking at the floor. What could he say to this brother he'd just attempted to rob at gunpoint? Thanks just didn't seem to do it. Studying the floor for a while longer, the big man cleared his throat. "Thank you," he said, and walked down the stairs. He turned back and looked at Gerard once more. "Thank you again."

Gerard could hear the tears in the man's voice. "Just don't go holding nobody else up. Try a little faith in God and then have some faith in yourself." Then Gerard turned his back. This time he had nothing to fear.

Ray arrived at Georgette's around nine forty-five. He was apologetic for having made her wait so long. She could sense a bit of tension between them but once he gave her a hug, everything seemed to fall into place.

"So, what you been up to since I've been gone?" he asked.

"I watched some of the Sixers game, then I did some meditating to Luther and the likes. And after all that strenuous activity, I needed to take a bath." She grinned, raising her eyebrows.

"Oh, that's right, we were supposed to go to the game tonight, huh? I'm sorry about that." He took a deep breath and sat down on the plush sofa. "I'm worn out, Georgette, but if you want to do something this evening I'm sure I can muster up some extra energy."

"No, this is fine. I'm somewhat tired myself. How about watching a few movies while you make dinner?" she teased.

"Are you hungry? Okay, what you got in there to fix?" he said, rising from the sofa. She grabbed his hand and pulled him back down on the couch.

"I was joking, Ray, you don't have to cook. Besides, I ate already. Are you hungry?" He was looking at her with his head half cocked. He grinned a slow smile, then ruffled her hair.

"There, that's better. Now you look like you've been home lounging around instead of on your way out on a date."

She repeated his same actions, only Ray was too fast. Refusing to give up the battle, she stood up in front of him until she could get both hands on his head. He was leaning further and further away, trying to escape contact. Finally he had to yield, because his back was flat on the left side of the sofa. Laughing, Georgette knelt down beside him as he tried to tie up her hands with his. After a tedious effort, she gave up. Breathing hard, she sat down on the sofa next to him. He gently pulled her toward him, directing her to lay her head on his chest. She obliged as he put both hands around her shoulders.

"You know, Georgette, this has been one crazy weekend, but if I had to do it all over again I would. Maybe not everything, but being here with you and all."

What a sweet thing to say, she thought. "Yes it has been nice. How are you feeling about me really? How do you feel about your cousin and me?" she asked.

He didn't say anything for a long time.

Mainly because it was such a complicated situation. "I still feel the same way about you today as I did when we first met on the slopes in Vail, only closer. I don't know, sweetheart, I don't want to be forced to make a choice. Do you think it will come to that?" he asked.

"I'm not sure, Ray. Sometimes I feel like this is too much to deal with and other times I feel like it's no big deal. I would never force you to make a choice, but I'm sure there will be times when I need you to let me know what you think about all this stuff and about your cousin." She leaned further into him. "By the way, is she pregnant for sure?" She really didn't want to know, but felt compelled to ask anyway.

He hesitated deliberately, searching for the right words to say. "Yeah," he said, squeezing her tighter. He didn't want to ruin the mood. Tonight would be their last night together. "Tell you what," he continued. "Let's not talk about that right now, okay?"

"I don't know. It depends," she responded.

"Depends? On what?"

"On whether or not I have your undivided attention for the rest of this weekend. We have what's left of tonight and all day tomorrow." She turned to look at him face to face.

"You've got it. I'm all yours if you can handle it," he teased, tilting her chin up to the level of his lips. *Oh my goodness,* she thought, closing her eyes. The kiss seemed to last forever and ever. She needed to come up for air but he wouldn't allow it. That was okay, she thought. Right now she needed him more than she needed air itself.

Eighteen

Georgette's face was beaming when she walked into her office on Monday morning. She had arrived before everyone else; she was happy about that. She wanted some time to switch gears. She knew that Anne would be ribbing her all day about her "attitude adjustment." Leaning back against the chair, her hands on the desk, she wondered what Ray was thinking about this morning. She had hated to see him leave the previous night, but she knew that all play and no work wasn't how the real world functioned. She could hear Anne's voice through the elevator doors before they even reached their floor.

"Hey, girl!" her secretary said, rushing into Georgette's office. "Looks like you've been struck by a lightning bolt . . . or *rod*. Which one was it?" She laughed, plopping down in the chair. All Georgette could do was grin.

"Guess it was the *Magnum!*" Anne joked.

"All I will say, Anne, is that I am rocking and rolling again." She laughed, high-fiving her secretary.

"Well, girl, I ain't gonna get in all your business, but it is damn time we saw you smiling again."

"Thanks, Anne. You've been a great source of . . . inspiration." Georgette smiled.

"Just remember that around evaluation time, okay?" she said, laughing as she walked out of the office. She paused at the doorway. "And Georgette, welcome back."

The smell of soaked sweat pants and the sight of bare arms protruding from loose T-shirts met Ray as he entered the gym. The air was heavy inside. It always took awhile for Ray's body to adjust to the lack of fresh air. Everybody working out had a different grunt, move, and facial expression to offer him as he walked by.

Staying fit was hard work, especially for the brothers at Slappy's Gym. The gym had acquired the name because its owner, Fred Smalls, better known as Smitty, made a practice of running around slapping brothers wherever he felt they needed to work out most. Ray recalled his first day at the gym like it was yesterday. As he did his squats, toting fifty-pound weights, Ray flinched as Smitty ran by and slapped him in the stomach. "You need to do some more crunches, son, if you want to rid yourself of those three months," he remembered the man saying.

The brother standing next to him had noticed his agitation and told him that Smitty was the owner and meant no harm. It was his way of interacting with his clients. From that day on, he had become a member of the club, Slappy's, which represented brothers from the East, South, and West Side of Chicago, all of whom had been at one time or another slapped by Smitty Smalls.

Ray was feeling hyped. He felt like he could pump iron all day. He was in love with Philly, the weekend, and a certain Georgette Willis. If he had his druthers, she would be the next and last Mrs. Fuschée.

"Over here, Ray!" Ali motioned from the bench-press machines.

"Hey now," Ray said, giving up the handshake.

"How was your trip to Philly?"

Ray shook his head and smiled widely. "What a phenomenal weekend! A blissful, wonderful trip, minus a few situations here and there."

"I heard you saw Lynn and her man, who also happened to be old girl's ex," Ali revealed.

Ray raised an eyebrow at his cousin. "Boy, news sure does get around fast. Man, it was crazy. For a minute, I thought I was going to have to slay homey. The way he treated Georgette—I've never seen anything like it in all my many years."

"You mean to tell me nobody had any idea who was who? That's weird, man! It's too close for comfort, if you ask me."

"Well, Ali, I ain't asking, I'm just doing, you know?"

"That's cool, Ray, but let me ask you this. Has Georgette resolved her feelings about her ex? Did you ask her that?"

Ray found himself becoming defensive but knew his cousin meant no harm.

"No, we didn't really get a chance to discuss that. Basically, we addressed the problem with her and Lynn and my being able to deal with it, if at all."

Ali sat up and wiped his face. He studied his cousin for a short time and said, "If you say everything is cool then everything is. I just want you to make sure it's a done deal with her and old boy, that's all. The truth is, I don't want her disrespecting you like Rachel did."

"Thanks, Ali, I appreciate that. But I think this one is for real."

"I certainly hope so, my man. Is this girl Georgette, degree-struck like Rachel was?"

"What do you mean by that?" Ray asked.

"Come on, Ray, you know what I mean. Is she hung up on the education thing? Does it matter to her? Do you know if she's ever dated someone without a degree?"

"I don't know, what are you getting at? I have my associate's. That's taken me where I wanted to go. She'll either accept me the way I am with regard to my 'credentials,' or she won't."

"But what has she said about the four-year thing? You said she graduated from Howard University and that she's an editor for the local print media. I figured she must be prone to men with paper. Do you detect that at all?"

Ray was silent. He was thinking about his and Georgette's past conversations and whether or not they ever dealt with the degree issue. He was sure his status in that department was all right with her; if it hadn't been, they wouldn't have gotten this far. He didn't feel that she was the type to judge a person on appearances or status. But he was slightly concerned about Ali's words. Georgette was an educated and successful woman who was often in the company of intelligent, progressive, polished men. He wondered if she ever had doubts about his background . . . The thought had never really occurred to him. Ray gazed at his cousin directly. "To be straight up, Ali, I don't really know, but I know she wants me for me. That's why I like her."

"I hear you. So, you kept some energy on reserve to hit the weights despite getting weak in the legs this past weekend?" Ali laughed as he rose from the bench to trade places with Ray.

Ray merely returned the smile and lay

back. After about six reps, he took a slight break, then started again.

"So, when do I get to meet this babydoll?" Ali asked.

"Soon," Ray said, straining between reps.

"Really? Is she coming this way?"

"Next month." Ray sat up to catch his breath. "I invited her out here for the holiday weekend."

"Who's springing for the ticket?"

"I am, of course."

"Sounds serious. You two plan on maintaining a long-distance relationship? How you going to keep that up?"

"The best way we can, I suppose. It's too early to know for sure, but I'll give it a spin if she's willing to. I know one thing, I'd rather spend money on a plane ticket than run up the kind of phone bills we've been seeing. She'll come out here next month for a weekend and I'll go out there the following month to visit her for a weekend. We already agreed to it."

"Is that right? That must be some powerful stuff she's serving you. I hope it's a long-term thing for you."

"Yeah? Well, we shall see now, won't we?" Ray smiled.

Preoccupied with thoughts of why Georgette had disliked Cheryl, Gerard walked past Vivian silently.

"Good morning, Mr. Jenkins," the woman greeted pleasantly.

Normally Gerard would have stopped to ask his secretary how her weekend was, but Gerard was comparing Cheryl to Georgette.

"Hi," he responded in a dry tone.

Reclining in the almond-colored leather swivel chair, he loosened his tie. Most of the senior executives were attending a meeting in New York. For the next few days he could loosen up somewhat. He was glad they were gone. The recent events of his life were starting to have a detrimental effect on him. He needed a shave and a haircut. He would schedule an appointment with the barber tomorrow and make an appointment with the manicurist later on in the week.

Gerard tried to get his mind off Georgette but couldn't, Cheryl Lynn Gray had waged a war against the woman he realized he still loved. The buzzer went off on the phone, interrupting his thoughts.

"Mr. Jenkins, there is a Ms. Gray for you on line one. Do you want to take the call?"

What he wanted was for Vivian to address him as Gerard instead of Mr. Jenkins. But she wouldn't hear of it. It had something to do with her upbringing, her residing and working in England for many years. That's the way things were done in England, he guessed. Nobility, royalty, honor, all that stuff was important to her. Snapping back to the situation at hand, he closed his eyes. He didn't want to speak with Cheryl, not now, not tomorrow, not ever. Resting forward on his elbows, he pressed the intercom button and responded, "No, Vivian, I do not wish to accept the call. Tell her I'm in a meeting, in the bathroom, whatever you like. Thanks."

He wished he would have understood his feelings for Georgette earlier and why Cheryl was a poor replacement. He had never really understood why Georgette despised Cheryl so. The look in her eyes this past weekend, when the two women had come face to face! Reflecting for the tenth time on the weekend's events, he desperately wished that Cheryl wasn't pregnant. Gerard stood up and stretched. He was starting to feel overwhelmed with anxiety. He had to remember the vision and believe. Acknowledge that and everything in his life would be all right. He knew what he had to do.

Lifting the receiver, he dialed some numbers. He should have placed this call before now.

"Good morning, this is the *Globe*. How may I help you?"

"Georgette Willis, please," he said in an authoritative voice.

"May I tell her who's calling?" Gerard hesitated, but only for a moment. This was part of the plan, the vision. "Yes, tell her it's Gerard Jenkins."

"It's Gerard," she murmured to Georgette from the doorway.

Georgette's heart jumped into overdrive. *My God,* she thought, *why is he calling me?* She glanced at Anne for some advice.

"Do you want to talk to him?" Anne asked.

"Should I? I wonder what he wants?" Her hands were beginning to shake now.

"Well, the only way to find out is to face the music," Anne advised.

Georgette's head was swimming. She was being bombarded by all of the stored emotions from the last few months. If it had been a few months ago, she would have welcomed the call, appreciated the effort. Now it seemed too late. She was moving on with her life the best way she knew how.

What did he want to say to her? Did he think she would want to hear any of his sorry excuses or meaningless apologies? *Please,* she thought. She had heard it all before and all too often. Basically, his time was up. It didn't matter if he huffed and he puffed and he threatened to blow her house down. The bottom line was, somebody else has been sleeping in her bed.

Marvin Gaye's "Let's Get It On" was piping over the phone lines while Gerard patiently waited. He knew Georgette was trying to decide whether or not to accept his call.

He took a deep breath, then wiped his brow with his handkerchief. He would understand if she didn't pick up. Why would she? He didn't know what he was going to say to her, anyway. He wasn't sure if he liked his reformed behavior. He found himself acting first, thinking later. If he got Georgette back, everything would be back to normal. He'd lead a good life, go to church, stay faithful, anything, anything to have Georgette back. It had been five minutes since the secretary answered the call. Chances were, Georgette had decided to leave him hanging. Well then, he would hang.

Taking a deep breath, Georgette reached for the flashing red button. She lifted the receiver.

"Yes, Gerard," she uttered evenly. She didn't want to give him the satisfaction of sensing her agitation.

"Hello, Georgette. How you doing?" he said softly.

"Fine," she said simply. "What do you want Gerard?"

"I need to talk to you. Can we meet somewhere today?"

No way! Georgette thought, breaking the number two pencil she held in half. "We're talking now. What do you want?" she asked again.

She was going to make this difficult. What could he possibly say to her to make her want to meet with him? After a moment's silence he said, "Listen, you're at work and I'm at work and I really think now is not the time. Would you at least consider meeting me somewhere? I can call you back later or tomorrow."

"Honestly, Gerard, you don't need to call me at all. What is worth discussing that would require a face-to-face meeting? You aren't calling to tell me you have AIDS or something, are you?"

"What? Of course not, Georgette. Why you even asking me that?"

"Because if it isn't, then it's nothing I have to see you about. So you take care of yourself."

Slam! There, it was done, she had the last word and felt victorious. The phones were ringing out of control now but Anne did manage to give her the thumbs-up sign.

"Whew!" she uttered, taking another deep breath. Now all she could hope for was that she didn't start obsessing about what Gerard wanted to talk to her about. She wanted to call her confidante, her soror, her honcho: Melinda. But Georgette was trying to practice restraint. She didn't want to disturb Melinda with every little detail of her personal life as soon as it occurred. Melinda had her own problems, with Don trying to make a comeback. Georgette hoped that he was serious and not just trying to strike back at Melinda for dumping him three years ago.

Georgette felt the pressure in her eyes and knew she was about to get a killer headache. She hated to admit it, but she still cared for Gerard, even missed him somewhat. She shook her head, as if the movement might put an abrupt end to such thoughts. She deliberated to herself that there would be no way she would allow Gerard Jenkins back into her life. But heading toward the restroom, Georgette couldn't help but feel that her life was about to get even more complicated.

Nineteen

For the next several weeks, Georgette worked out an average of three to four times a week. She wanted to be in tiptop shape when she saw Ray that weekend. She didn't like the fact that her waistline was still measuring twenty-eight inches after all the twists, turns, and calorie counting. But she guessed it was better than the thirty inches she had measured five weeks ago. Her hips still measured thirty-eight inches easily.

Flipping through the *Jet* magazine at the hair salon, she wondered how come every centerfold woman *Jet* ever displayed managed to have measurements of 36-24-36. "Please," she said, slamming the magazine shut. Her outburst was drowned out by the hum of blow-dryers and the music on the CD player at Silky's Salon.

"What's up, slim?" André, her hairdresser, said, flinging a cape at her.

"Hey, André, I've got a serious situation going on this weekend so give me the works,"

Georgette replied, easing into a soft mauve leather chair.

"You're looking supreme, girl! So, what've you been doing?" he asked, snapping the cape behind her neck.

"Working out. Why? Can you really notice?"

"I notice everything, sweetheart. It's my job. What you having done today?"

"Touch up and trim. Just a basic trim, okay?" she said.

He nodded. "You wearing it up or down?" he asked.

She thought about it for a moment. Factoring in the weather conditions in Chicago this time of the year, she decided to wear it down. It was May. The temperature would be just right there, not too humid and not too cold. She was happy that it was a three-day weekend. Her job had taken its toll on her the past few weeks, with all the article submissions, rewrites, and interviews. Not to mention the bombardment of phone calls by Gerard.

She had put the word out to Anne not to accept any of his calls. Certainly after Anne told him that she had been sent on assignment to Siberia, he would get the hint. But he just kept trying, once, twice, sometimes three times a week. At her home, at the office, it didn't seem to matter. Gerard was hell-bent on talking to her. He barraged her with more flowers in three weeks than he had during the entire time they were dating. Perhaps he had finally caught the clue, though, because things were quiet this week. Maybe he sensed it was a lost cause. Or maybe he had found his peace. Whatever the case, Georgette admitted she missed the attention.

"There! You're all beautiful again," André teased, handing her the mirror to check out the back of her hair.

"Looking good!" She smiled, reaching into her wallet to get some cash. He had given her curly hair a nice trim. André had hooked it up, giving her a bouncing-and-behaving hairdo with the left side hanging over her left eye.

"Where are you headed this weekend, Ms. Thing?" inquired André.

"Chicago."

"Really? I've got some family in Chi-town. Say hello to them for me—that's if you have the time," he teased. The salon was small but the mouths were huge. She had become paranoid since the situation with Ray and Cheryl. You never know who knows who, she thought. She handed him three twenties and a ten. "Thanks, Dré. I'll see you in two weeks. Stay out of trouble."

Stepping out of the salon, she thought to herself, *Get ready, Ray, cause here I come . . .*

* * *

Gerard was propped up against the Honda Accord as Georgette made her way to the parking lot. She was searching for those keys again and hadn't noticed him there, resting on her car. "Hi, Georgette," he said, startling her. That will teach her to have her keys out before reaching the car, he thought. He didn't know how many times he had warned her about searching for her keys in a parking lot. "I see you still believe in walking and digging for your keys at the same time," he joked.

Georgette didn't laugh. She narrowed her eyes at him. "What do you think you're doing?"

"I figured you might have missed all the calls and flowers this week, so I wanted to give you these." Pulling his arm from behind him, Gerard handed her a dozen white long-stemmed roses. Clamping her eyes shut in frustration, she thought to herself, *Don't lose it, girl, even if these are your favorite flowers.* "What are you doing here?"

"I know you usually go to the salon every other Thursday. When you weren't here last week, I took my chances that you'd be here today. Of course, I cruised the parking lot this time to be sure." He pushed the flowers toward her again.

"I can't accept these, Gerard."

"Oh? Why not? They're your favorite." In

a panic, he realized things weren't going as he'd planned.

"Gerard, what do you want?" she said, pushing him to the side as she attempted to put the key in the hole. He stood firm. "Could you please move out of the way?" she demanded.

"What is it that I want? I want you back, Georgette." There, he finally got the opportunity to say what he had been wanting to say, needing to say, for weeks.

Georgette was silent. She didn't even look up at him. She kept her head bowed to the ground, trying not to respond. Her heart was doing that jumping, pumping, and thumping thing again. He was standing too close and smelling too good.

"Georgette," he said, "I know I've hurt you. I know you don't want to hear or believe anything I have to say. But you need to know and believe that I miss you and I still love you very much. I can't sleep. I can hardly finish a meal without thinking about you. There isn't a day that goes by that I don't long to be near you. Seems like I can't breathe without you. Okay, I know I screwed up, but I swear on my father's grave if you give me a second chance to make things right, I'll never hurt you again. I swear," he pleaded.

"A second chance? You mean a fourth or fifth chance, don't you?" She was staring him in the eyes now. "Furthermore, how dare you swear on your dad's grave. God bless his soul, but he has nothing to do with your sorry behavior!" She was standing in his face now. "Gerard, I don't want to get into it with you, okay? Let's just part ways and call it a done deal."

"I know I've hurt you and I know you've given me chance after chance. I know I've abused those chances. But I'm a changed person now, Georgette, I promise you. I can't just turn off my feelings for you like that. We've been through too much for so long."

"Oh really? You seemed to turn them off just fine while you were out there making a baby."

He hung his head back and took a deep breath. *Touché*. She had stuck it to him where it hurt the most. He wanted to tell her about Cheryl and how foolish he was. But the timing wasn't right.

"What do you want me to do, Georgette? Just name it and I'll do it!"

She studied his face for a minute. He was serious this time, she could tell. But she was in no mood to be forgiving or accommodating. She turned her back, bent down, and tried to open the car door again. This time he moved out of her way.

"Just name it!" he begged.

She had mustered up the strength and courage over the past few months to say exactly what was on her mind, no matter what the consequences. Glancing back at him, she said simply, "Unscrew Cheryl."

He shook his head, then dropped his face in his hands. "I'm sorry, Georgette! Please, can't we even try to work out something?"

"I just told you what you needed to do," she said. *That should do it,* she thought, turning her back to open the car door. She snatched the flowers out of his hands and threw them in the passenger seat.

Gerard quickly moved to close the gap between them. In a moment, she could feel his breath on her neck and his body pressed against hers.

"Back up, Gerard," she ordered, turning to face him. But he didn't move. She could feel herself slipping and he could feel it, too. Placing both his hands on the roof of the car, he boxed her in. He pressed up close against her body. He could feel her breasts with his chest. She could feel his breath on her skin. She was almost lost, but then something snapped her back to reality. Ducking from under his arms, she stepped into the car. She opened the sunroof and the window, then closed the door. He knelt down and looked into the car.

"Can't I stop by later?" he asked.

Damn! she thought, *what's happening here?* Clearing her throat, she said firmly, "No. I have something to do."

His eyes were pleading now. "How about

we go up to the Vineyard this weekend? We could spend some time together, set things straight. I promise not to touch you if you don't want me to."

Cheap trick, she thought. He knew good and well how much she loved the Vineyard. It had been their romantic getaway on so many occasions . . .

"I'm going out of town this weekend." She could tell by his expression that he was wondering if she was going to see Ray.

"Where are you going?" he asked softly.

"To see a friend." Why was she trying to spare his feelings? He had never thought to protect hers.

"Chicago?" he asked. He hoped and prayed she would say no. He knew that Chicago was where Cheryl's cousin lived. Dammit! Why was Georgette going to see him? He fought to remain calm. Perhaps he was letting his imagination run away with him. Maybe she was going to visit her sister in Virginia for the Memorial Day weekend. But something within him told him that she wasn't heading for Virginia. Or for New York or Connecticut, for that matter. His feelings told him that she was flying to Chicago to see what's-his-name.

"You guessed it," she said. She couldn't help but feel a glimmer of satisfaction.

He could feel his adrenaline kicking in as he thought to himself, she better not have slept with him already. "Going to see what's-his-name?" he asked in a serious voice.

"Ray?" she said, toying with him now. "Yes. He invited me out for the weekend."

"Are you sleeping with him?" He shouldn't have asked the question because he knew he wasn't prepared for the answer. If she said yes, he would yank her out of the car. If she said no, more than likely he would still make a scene. But she said nothing. Not a damn thing!

She looked at him and smiled. *Got him!* Georgette thought. Now he knows how it feels. "I've gotta go. I haven't packed yet and I'm leaving tomorrow." She was being ruthless now. She cranked the ignition and released the emergency brake.

Gerard stood up and took a step back. Bending down again he said, "What if I asked you—no, begged you—not to go?"

Looking him straight in the eye, she leaned over. She motioned him with her index finger to come closer. Obligingly, he stepped forward. She motioned for him to come even closer, until his face was almost touching hers. Then she closed her eyes and placed a kiss on his lips. Surprised, Gerard tried desperately to engulf her tongue before she pulled away. Backing away slowly, she responded, "I'm sorry, Gerard."

He moved back in exactly enough time to avoid the tires from rolling over his feet. As he stood up he watched the little silver car as it blended into traffic. Slowly walking over to the Jeep, he turned back once again. She was gone; the only thing left was her scent on his lips. He felt like he had just had the wind knocked out of him. He couldn't make heads or tails out of the kiss. Why did she kiss him? Was she playing a game, or what? He had never known her to be the game-playing type. Though lately he couldn't seem to figure anything right. That was okay, though, because he wasn't going to give up. He would win her back if it took his last breath.

Twenty

Ray was awaiting Rachel's phone call. He wanted to wrap up this insurance thing as soon as possible. He needed Anthony's social security number so he could list his son as his sole beneficiary.

He was also thinking about making a will, just to make sure Rachel wouldn't get her grubby little paws on anything if anything ever happened to him. One of the brothers at the gym had told him about an uncle who hadn't taken the time to change his policies after his divorce. Five years, a new wife, and two children later, he died, leaving his family with nothing. All of the insurance policies listed his first wife.

After hearing that story, Ray realized the importance of setting the record straight. He scheduled an appointment with his brother's girlfriend to make out a simple will. Maxine, a paralegal, provided basic services such as wills, trusts, bankruptcy, and restraining orders at reasonable rates.

Ray had a list of things to do before the

day ended, including stopping by the grocery store to pick up some food for the weekend. He was thrilled about Georgette's visit and wanted to make sure that everything went well. He had cleaned the apartment the previous night, with the help of Joe, vacuuming, dusting, washing, soaking, and scrubbing. The place was spotless.

He managed to convince Joe to stay at Maxine's for the weekend. Honestly, it wasn't that hard for him to bribe his baby brother to do anything related to his happiness. Joe gladly accepted the proposition because he wanted the weekend to go just as well as Ray did. Joe even purchased a bottle of Möet for the occasion. He would pick up some fresh flowers for the table tomorrow. He wanted to make sure the dinner would be superb and the ambiance perfect. When the phone rang, he braced himself for a possible altercation with his ex. "Hello?"

"Ray, this is Rachel." She read the social security number to him as fast as she could and continued, "Anthony's been asking for you the last few nights. Do you want to have him this weekend?"

Ray knew the only reason Rachel would agree to let him have Anthony was if she had something she wanted to do. Ray was careful in his reply because he didn't want her to suspect anything. She had been acting strangely the last two weeks. He couldn't put his hands on it, but he knew she was up to something. She had been calling just about every other day, trying to set up a so-called family day with the three of them. When he went to pick Anthony up the previous weekend, she had invited him to stay for the night. He kindly turned her down and got the hell out of there. Blame it on the full moon or whatever, but she was acting strange. He cleared his throat and replied, "I've got a lot of things to take care of this weekend. How about one night next week?"

"You can't take Anthony with you while you take care of these so-called things?"

"Rachel, I can't do it, that's all. I've got a lot on my plate, all right?" He wasn't going to be manipulated by her. "Sounds to me like you're trying to get rid of him for the weekend. What's on your agenda?" He put the ball back in her court.

"Nothing. He's been asking for you, that's all," she replied.

There was a moment of silence and then she said, "So, what are you doing this weekend? You have a gig somewhere?" He wasn't about to answer her questions about his personal life.

"Shoot! My pager is flashing. I gotta go, it looks like it's the firehouse. I'll talk to you later. Tell Anthony I'm off on Tuesday and I'll pick him up in the morning, okay?" He didn't wait for an answer. She was digging a little too deep. He hated to use the department as an excuse, but what else was he supposed to do? She wouldn't retreat.

Now all he had left to do was oil his saxophone, pick up some scented candles and, last but not least, pick up the Luther Vandross tickets. This was going to be a weekend Georgette would never forget, he thought, locking the door behind him.

"I don't know what to pack. What do you think the weather is like? Do you think I should take my suede jacket or the leather one?"

"Slow down, Georgette, why don't you," Melinda advised over the phone.

"Okay, okay, it's just that I'm feeling overwhelmed, that's all."

"Overwhelmed by what? You said you got your hair and nails done, your pedicure and your traveler's checks, right? So what else is left to do?"

"I'm all done except for the packing part. I guess I have a few more hours, so I should just chill, right?"

"Right! Just pipe it down a notch or two. What time is your flight leaving?"

"Four-thirty P.M."

"Girl, please! You've got damn near all day tomorrow to pack if you need to. How are things with you and Ray? Is it getting serious, or what?"

"I don't know, I'm taking it one day at a time. I had to get that Cheryl thing under control."

"I can understand it. Have you seen her anymore?" Melinda asked.

"Not since that night. I went to the sorority meeting last Saturday but she wasn't there. Although I did see Gerard today."

"You did? Get out of here, where?"

"In the parking lot at Silky's."

"What happened?" Melinda wanted to make sure her girlfriend was all right. Georgette had already told her about Gerard's phone calls and the flowers and she seemed to be handling things fine. But today was the first time Georgette had actually seen Gerard since the whole escapade took place.

"He was waiting at my car when I came out."

"Stop it!"

"He was there with a dozen white long-stemmed roses." Georgette recapped the scene between her and Gerard. Melinda was silent as she heard Gerard's promises and Georgette's replies.

"How's your heart holding up?" Melinda questioned.

"I'm fine, really."

God forgive her, but she didn't want to tell her best friend her true feelings. The reality was that she missed Gerard. The way he stood breath to breath with her, the way all those feelings surged up inside her, the way he vowed to stay true to her.

But how could she let go of the pain and hurt he had caused? He had disappointed her too many times. Georgette had to let him go. Anything else was impossible. Besides, Georgette knew she was falling in love with Ray. She also knew that she couldn't stay in love with two men for much longer. She would have to let Gerard go, for now, anyway. After all, she could confidently say to herself, she had been there and done that with regards to Gerard. Awaiting her was a smooth chocolate brother named Ray and boy, oh, boy, how she wanted him to make her day!

The sun, shining clear and bright this morning, was reflecting off Lake Michigan as Ray finished up his last lap. He needed to clear his mind before he started his day. The anticipation of Georgette's arrival was driving him crazy. He had completed everything he needed to do, with the exception of getting a haircut. The barber would be open early as usual, but he knew the shop would be extra crowded because of the upcoming holiday weekend.

Ray arrived a few minutes past eight. Looking into the door window, he could see Jamal in the back changing his top. Jamal always wore smocks made out of Kente cloth, mud cloth, or some other type of African fabric. Seeing Ray's face at the glass door window, Jamal gave him a "wait a second" gesture and a smile. Other brothers were starting to line up behind Ray. This was going to be a long day and some long pay for Jamal.

"Greetings in the name of Allah, brothers," Jamal said, grinning as he opened the door.

"How you doing, Jamal?" Ray said, sitting down in the African cane barber chair.

"I'm doing fine, my brother. What you have, man?"

"The usual. Not too much off the sides and a little lower on the top."

"What's everybody doing for the holiday weekend?" Jamal asked, glancing around at the young men in the shop. Noncommittal remarks issued from the others, but Ray, whose cup runneth over with excitement, shared his plans with Jamal.

"Sounds like you have a nice time lined up. Just don't forget to saddle up," Jamal said matter-of-factly. "These diseases ain't nothing to be messing around with. Maybe if you young brothers could stop chasing the women for a minute, you could come down to the mosque and learn a few things."

"I hear what you're saying Jamal, but don't

worry. I've got it all taken care of." Ray smiled.

Ray arrived home and immediately turned on the radio on his stereo. Turning to the local jazz station, he jumped into the shower. He stood under the water for a long time, rolling his shoulders and head back and forth. He let the hot water beat down on his neck and back until he felt limp. He gave himself two good washings, then rinsed his hair for a final time. Using a small hand towel, he dried his body. He didn't want to use the new towels because they were there for a more deserving purpose, along with the candles.

Slipping into some black silk boxers, he walked into the L-shaped kitchen and plugged in the mini food processor. He needed to chop some garlic, green peppers, red peppers, and onions. Setting the ingredients on a saucer, he turned on the cold water. Placing the jumbo shrimp under the running water, he began the laborious task of peeling and de-veining them. He put the shrimp in a small bowl then sprinkled some curry powder and lemon juice on them. He set the box of angel hair pasta next to the stove.

He then sliced some zucchini, yellow squash, mushrooms, and more yellow onions and set them in another bowl in the refrigerator. He would use the white oyster sauce to flavor the vegetables. The Moët was already chilling, along with the champagne glasses.

Unfolding the floral tablecloth, he placed it over the maple table. His grandmother had given him the table when he moved out on his own at seventeen. He centered the vase in the middle of the table. All he needed to do now was pick up some exotic flowers before Georgette's arrival. He already had the candles set in the brass holders and had borrowed the orange cloth napkins to offset the orange in the table cloth from his sister Theresa.

Finally, the mood had been set. He would start the potpourri burner on his way to the airport so that the house would be filled with fragrance on their return.

There was one more thing he had to do to put the finishing touches on the evening. He wanted to program the CD player. With CDs scattered all over the floor, he loaded the first magazine with Walter Beasley, Kim Waters, Gerald Albright, Joe Sample, Fatburger, and Fourplay. He loaded the second magazine with the Whispers, Angela Bofill, Will Downing, Oleta Adams, Phil Perry, and the soundtrack from the movie *Boomerang*.

Only a few hours stood between him and the woman he was falling deeply in love with. He laid out his attire on the purple sheets and then folded the comforter across the foot of the bed. He would have to remember to place a rose on her side of the bed. Changing the bedroom light bulbs from a bright white to a soft yellow, he took a deep breath.

"Everything will be just fine," he said to himself, glancing around the bedroom once more to make sure everything was perfect. Needing to regain his strength, he fell across the bed and closed his eyes. Ali and Joe would meet them at the show tonight. He sensed the anticipation by his brother, cousin, and selected friends because everyone wanted to meet "Ms. Georgette." He had done a good job by lining up top-shelf seats for the Luther Vandross concert tonight. Georgette didn't have a clue as to their plans. After all she's been through, she deserved a surprise and some special treatment this weekend. He decided to take it upon himself to personally see to it that she had one of the most memorable times of her life.

Repositioning his body, he laid his forearm over his eyes. Maybe he should set the alarm to make sure he didn't oversleep. Yeah, right, he smiled, rolling over. Like he really needed an alarm clock to wake him up tonight.

After the third knock, Gerard searched the driveway one more time to make sure the Honda was gone. Mr. Burke looked out the window and yelled down to Gerard, "What do you want, young fellow?"

"I'm trying to reach Georgette, I need to speak with her. Do you know where she is?"

"You just missed her. She pulled out of here, oh, about twenty or thirty minutes ago. Say, what's your name?"

Gerard, fighting hard to keep his face from showing disappointment, replied, "Gerard."

"Okay then, Gerard, I'll tell her you dropped by when she gets back. Now don't go banging on that there door no more, all right?" Mr. Burke closed the window before he could respond.

Gerard sat in the car for a minute, trying to collect his thoughts. Should he catch a flight out to Chicago and bring her back? Wait a minute, he thought. He didn't know how or where to find her. The only person who had any information on Ray was Cheryl. Maybe she would provide him with her cousin's last name and possibly his phone number. Even if she wouldn't give him the number he could at least call information and ask for it once he had the last name.

What to do, what to do? he thought, stopping at the light. He hadn't returned any of Cheryl's calls in two weeks. How was he supposed to approach her now? He would take his chances and go by her house. What else was there left for him to do?

"Who is it?" Cheryl asked in a groggy voice.

"It's Gerard," he said, leaning his shoulder against the door.

"Wait a minute," she said, racing to the bathroom to check her look in the mirror. Luckily for her, she had cleaned the apartment from top to bottom the night before last. It had been a little over a month since she had last seen Gerard. She was wearing a maternity smock and matching skirt. Her hair was pinned up in a twist. She quickly reapplied some lipstick and went back to the door. Opening the door, she was surprised to see how haggard he looked. For the first time since she'd known Gerard, he had dark circles beneath his eyes.

"Hi, Cheryl, how you doing?" Golly, he thought, she was looking positively radiant. She had what they called the glow. Her skin was clear, her face full, happy. Her stomach was starting to divulge its little secret. He could feel something else stirring inside of him as he stared at her middle.

Noticing the way he was staring at her, she grabbed his hand and led him inside. Placing his hands on her stomach, she said, "This is junior. Junior, this is your daddy."

Gerard stood there for a moment, surprised by the feeling of excitement. He was going to be a dad.

"Where have you been? I've been trying to call you for the last few weeks," she asked.

"I've been traveling, working hard." Gerard took a deep breath. He was lying again, something he had promised himself he wasn't going to do anymore. "To tell you the truth, Cheryl, I've been avoiding you. I've been avoiding this entire situation. I just didn't feel up to returning your calls."

She knew what he meant. "I see." A surge of jealousy for Georgette came rising up.

"So, what did your doctor say about the due date?"

"Funny you should bring that up. I just got back from my appointment about an hour ago. I'm due around October third."

He didn't say anything. He just nodded his head and kept silent.

"Gerard, I think we need to talk about this baby."

"What do you want to talk about? First names? Colors? What?"

"There is no need to be smart about this, okay? I was thinking more along the lines of last names."

This girl has lost her mind if she thinks he would even consider marrying her, Gerard thought. "What do you mean, last names? What's wrong with your last name?" he asked.

"Nothing. I thought maybe you would want the child to have your last name, that's all."

"My last name? And how are we supposed to go about doing that?"

She glared at him. "Well, are you planning on supporting the child?" she fired back.

He stood up; it was time to leave. He hadn't come there to be insulted. Replaying her question over in his head, he answered, "Of course I will! What kind of man do you take me for? You know, Cheryl, I didn't ask for, nor did I agree to having, this child. However, I will make sure that he or she will be provided for."

"Provisions? What about playing a key role in the child's upbringing? What? You're just going to drop off some money, diapers, or food at the doorstep and keep on going? Don't you even want to know your own child?"

"Calm down, Cheryl. I'm sure all this hostility isn't good for the baby."

"As if you even care about the child's well-being! *Please,*" she yelled.

Gerard headed for the door. He should never have come by unexpectedly. He should not have come by at all, for that matter. If there was one thing he didn't need it was another wild scene with Cheryl.

"Call me if you need anything for the baby. Like I said before, I will do my part," he said, walking out the door.

She looked surprised when he turned back

suddenly to face her. "By the way, how's your cousin Ray, what's his last name?" he asked.

"Fuschée," she said through tight lips.

"Yeah, whatever. How's he handling this?"

"He's handling it about as well as I am," she snarled, closing the door behind him.

That evening, Cheryl thought back on Gerard's visit. Why had he asked what Ray's last name was? Probably had something to do with that damn Georgette. She would have to give good ole Cousin Ray a call this weekend.

She had no intentions of getting all worked up again. The doctor told her she needed to take it easy because she ran the risk of going into labor prematurely. She had a prolapsed uterus, which could make the pregnancy problematic. The doctor mentioned that she might have to stop working soon and stay home. He didn't want her to take any chances. It was a miracle for her to have conceived in the first place, since she had partially blocked tubes, in addition to the prolapsed uterus. Despite the circumstances of her pregnancy, she knew this baby was a blessing.

Her parents accepted the news the best way they could. Surprisingly, her dad had seemed rather pleased about the idea of being a grandfather. Her mother would have been more thrilled if she had brought home a husband first and then a baby.

The scene with Gerard replayed in her mind as she caressed her middle. All he would do is pay for things for the baby, rather than be there for the baby, for her. All the drama over last names. With a pain to her heart, Cheryl realized what deep inside she knew all along: Gerard Jenkins would never marry her.

Twenty-one

Ray slipped into his brown linen slacks. After buttoning the mustard-colored linen short-sleeve shirt, he slid on his brown leather tasseled shoes over brown, gold, and burgundy patterned socks. He had a fetish for socks, all kinds, colors, and designs. Flipping through the neatly hung belts, he chose a soft brown cowhide one. He was scheduled to leave in fifteen minutes.

Looking in the bathroom mirror, he stroked his hair with a bristle brush. Perusing the many bottles of cologne neatly arranged on his vanity, he reached for the "JOOPS" bottle. Splashing the cologne on his neck, he looked around to make sure everything was in place.

Georgette would be his wife. He could feel the revelation stirring deep within his soul. He started the potpourri burner and headed out the door, driving straight to the airport to pick up the future Mrs. Fuschée.

* * *

Once inside the house, Gerard grabbed a pen and a sheet of paper. Snatching the cordless phone off its cradle, he sat down at his desk. This might be an all-night and all-day task, but he was determined—driven—to find Georgette and beg her to come back.

"Yes, operator, Chicago. I'm looking for a Ray Fuschée." He spelled the last name.

"Do you have a street address?" the operator drilled.

"No, I don't, ma'am. I seem to have misplaced it," he said.

"Let's see. Well, I don't find a Ray Fuschée. I have fourteen Fuschées throughout the Chicago area, and ten are listed."

Fourteen Fuschées? he thought to himself. How in the world could that be? It wasn't exactly a common name. Now what to do?

"Operator, I'll take all ten," he said. Carefully, Gerard wrote the numbers down on the sheet of paper. He repeated each number upon her completion. He didn't want to take any chances. He was going to get his angel back if he had to fly out there tomorrow to do it.

Georgette was wearing an ivory long-sleeved Lycra bodysuit, which had a pleated décolleté neckline. Exposing some skin, she had draped a few eighteen-inch Chanel crystal necklaces around her neck that matched

her earrings perfectly. The bodysuit smoothed
down tightly into the ankle-length red skirt.
The skirt had a fierce split up the middle,
tapering off about mid-thigh. She finished
off the outfit with a pair of red summer
suede sling-back pumps. Her nails were done
in the same barbecue red as her lips.

Ray spotted her right away among the
crowd. Sneaking up behind her, he slipped
his hands around her waist, bent over, and
rested his chin on top of her head.

"Hey, gorgeous!" he said, squeezing her
close.

"Hi, Ray," she said in her sexiest voice. She
dropped her bag to her side so that she could
free her hands. She wanted to make sure
nothing came between their bodies as she
stretched to give him a kiss. It was a long,
slow, tongue-entangling kiss. Forgetting about
the crowd of passengers, he allowed his hands
to roam tenderly around her back. It wasn't
until she felt his big, strong hands clenching
her thighs that she drew back. She took a deep
breath and cupped his hands.

"I almost forgot, we're in a public place,"
she said, wiping a trace of her lipstick from
his lips.

"So what?" he said, pulling her to his chest
again. "Just one more like that last one and
we can go."

"Ray," she protested. But before long, their

lips were attached again. After a few seconds, they resurfaced.

"We better go," she suggested.

"I think you're right. How was the flight?"

"Long and cramped, but well worth it," she said, grinning as she grabbed his free hand.

"I'm happy to hear that. Just wait until later," he twinkled. "You will have the best weekend of your life, I guarantee it!"

After the industrious walk through O'Hare, they eventually reached his blue Explorer.

Just as she thought, a Ford truck. She chuckled quietly.

"You want to share the joke?" he asked.

"It's not really a joke, it's more like a premonition. I knew you would have a Ford truck."

"Did you, now? Well, that goes to show you we're connecting. Now, all we need to do is get you to trade that Accord in and join the ranks of the real Americans."

"Forget you, Ray. I've got a real American for you."

"Is that right? We'll have to see about that!" he teased, closing her door.

Turning the key to the apartment, they were greeted by a rush of peach aroma. Georgette was immediately taken with his apartment. It was warm and inviting. The sofa faced a large window, which looked out over Lake Michigan.

"This is beautiful, Ray," she gasped.

"You like it?"

"I sure do!" she said, circling the dining room table. "Wow, who set this fabulous table?" she asked.

"Who do you think?"

"You? Get out of here! You have excellent taste, Mr. Fuschée," she said, walking over to examine the wrought-iron coffee table. This brother had it going on, she thought, living in a high rise on Lake Shore Drive. It was a picture-perfect setup. She felt like she was flipping through one of those architectural design magazines. He let her wander freely, taking in her facial expressions and body language.

"Can I see the rest of the place?"

"Of course," he said, and took her on a tour of the kitchen, then of Joe's bedroom and bathroom. Saving what he thought was the best for last, he opened his bedroom door.

The first thing she noticed was the high bed supported by oak pedestals and drawers. Then she saw the beautiful antique chest of drawers against the far wall.

"This is a one-of-a-kind piece here," she said, examining the chest with her hands.

"My grandmother gave it to me before she died. Her house was full of antiques that were divided among my family when she passed," he explained, walking back out of the room. "Are you hungry?"

"Kind of," she said, following behind him.

"Good! I've got a special meal planned."

He told her to get comfortable while he got things prepared. Remembering how much she enjoyed baths, he slipped away into the bathroom to run some water. He placed a few drops of scented bath oil under the running water until it bubbled up slightly. Then he lit the candles, braced in their blue wooden holders. Reaching under the sink, he pulled out a brown paper bag. Digging down into the bag, he clasped a handful of rose pedals and sprinkled them over the bathwater.

"Georgette, could you come here for a second?" he called. He could hear her heels clicking over the hardwood floor as she made her way into the bathroom.

How romantic, she thought, smiling to herself as she saw his shadow on the ceiling, flickering in the candlelight. "Ray, I can't believe it, all this for me?"

Instead of answering her, he began undressing her. When she was completely naked, he took a loving gaze at her curves and warm coloring then led her to the tub.

"Step in," he said invitingly. "Warm enough?" he asked as she snaked down slowly.

"It's perfect."

"Great! You relax here for a while. Dinner

will be ready in twenty or thirty minutes, all right? And by the way, we have a lot of things to do this evening."

He closed the door halfway and raced to the kitchen. It was seven P.M. and the concert started at nine-thirty. He wanted to arrive at least thirty minutes before the show to ensure ample parking. The Rosemont Horizon Center would be crowded, especially for this evening's performance.

Dinner was ready and the food was spread out on the table in half an hour.

"Georgette, it's time to eat, love," he called.

She was out in a flash, wearing one of his dress shirts with nothing underneath it.

He sighed, looking her over with his lips pressed together. Fighting the distraction she presented, he shook his head and blessed the table as Georgette looked on.

Twirling the pasta around her fork, she lifted it to her mouth. "Excellenté!" she exclaimed with her mouth full.

It was quiet for the next several minutes as Georgette entertained her palate with pieces of shrimp, pasta, zucchini, onion, and sips of Moët. It was already eight o'clock and Ray was feeling a bit stressed. The meal had been a success, with Georgette clearing her plate and returning for seconds. Wanting to keep the concert a surprise, he recommended she go change into something appropriate for an evening on the town. He informed her that they had exactly thirty minutes to get ready. She told him that it wouldn't take her that long. He wagered that he would be done before her. "I don't think so," she said, running into the bedroom. He quickly followed. The race was on!

Rachel was running late, as usual. It seemed like ever since Anthony was old enough to walk, she could never manage her time efficiently. Of all the nights to be behind schedule, she thought, pulling up to her parents' house.

Driving across town on a Friday night was a test of endurance in Chicago. The lights were already on as she carried Anthony out of the car. It was after his bedtime and he was already asleep. Dropping his bag on the ground, she spilled some of the contents.

"Rachel, is that you?" her mother asked, opening the front door.

"Yes, it's me, Mother. Sorry for being late. I had a lot of things to do before we came over here."

"That's fine. Is the baby asleep already?" Her mother took Anthony in her arms.

"Out like a light. I really appreciate this, Mom. I'll be back first thing tomorrow to pick him up. I put his asthma medicine in here just in case," she said, picking up the comb, brush, and asthma inhaler she had dropped on the ground.

"Where you going tonight, Rachel?"

"To see Luther Vandross."

"Who's accompanying you?"

"Gail and Donna are supposed to meet me there. I gotta go, Mom, I'm late," she said, kissing her mother on the forehead.

Late because of Ray, she added to herself. She wondered what the hell was so important that he couldn't take their son for the evening.

Suddenly she felt a surge of jealousy running through her body. Maybe that was because she hadn't addressed her feelings about Ray since the divorce. Deep down in her heart, she knew that if she had it to do over again, she would never risk losing Ray and the family unity they had. Even through all the fights, Ray was a good father and had been an ideal husband. She could see that now. But she knew it was too late. The damage had been done and nothing could ever make him trust her again.

The car immediately came to a stop once she turned the corner onto Main Street. The traffic awaiting to enter the parking lot was thick. "Damn," she huffed. She would miss the opening act if things didn't speed up. If only Ray could have helped her out this one time! Just wait until he comes to pick Anthony up on Tuesday.

* * *

Georgette still didn't have a clue as to what was going on as Ray parked the truck.

"Where are all these people going?" she asked.

"They are going to the same place we are," Ray grinned.

"And where is that?" she said, stretching her neck to see around the mammoth group of people.

"I don't know, Georgette," he said, parking the car. "Maybe they're going to the Luther Vandross concert."

"Luther! Ray, you didn't? Did you?"

"Well, like I said, I don't know. Do you like Luther?" he teased.

"Oh, Ray, are we going for real?" she asked.

"What did I tell you before? This is going to be the best weekend of your life. Now, let's go see Luther."

Opening her door, she leaped out on top of him, nearly tackling him to the ground. Hugging and kissing him all over his face, she said over and over again, "You're incredible. Thank you, Ray. Thank you."

Midway through the line, Rachel noticed a tall figure some fifty feet ahead of her. She immediately recognized the person. What she

didn't know was who the girl was he had
wrapped in his arms.

"I can't believe him!" she said in an irritated tone.

"What, Rachel? The fact that he's here or
the fact that he's with someone else?" Gail
quizzed.

"You don't know the half of it! I asked
his sorry self to watch Anthony tonight and
he gave me some lame excuse about being
preoccupied," she said, bobbing and weaving
her head around the people in front of her
so she could see. She wanted to keep close
tabs on Ray.

"I don't understand you, Rachel. I thought
you were happy to be rid of the man and
continuing on with your life," Donna pointed
out.

"If you ask me, Rachel, sounds like you
just want him because somebody else apparently has him. Or maybe since Doug dumped
you, you're secretly thinking or wishing you
could have Ray back," Donna continued.

"Donna, shut up!" Rachel warned.

Once they arrived home, Ray quickly began setting the mood for the remainder of
the evening. Luther Vandross had ignited
the night with his repertoire. And now,
Ray would cap the evening off with his.
Motioning Georgette to settle in for the

evening, he flipped on the stereo. Immediately humming out of the speakers was the saxophone sound of Kim Waters. While Georgette slipped into something more casual, Ray lit the candles he had strategically placed throughout the large bachelor pad. The room flickered with candlelight and the faint smell of fresh peaches laced the air.

Setting the bowl of strawberries and grapes on the end table next to the wrought-iron candleholders, he directed Georgette toward the sofa.

"Did you enjoy the concert?" he whispered, placing a strawberry in her mouth.

"I sure did, baby, it was outstanding. Did you see the way Luther's backup singers were dressed? Those girls were beautiful."

"Yeah, they were okay. But none of them compares to you," he moaned softly, kissing her on the lips.

"You're so sweet, Ray," she said, returning the kiss.

"You think so?" He smiled.

"With all my heart."

Ray rose from the sofa. "I want to show you something. I'll be right back. Go ahead and kick back."

Georgette posed on the sofa in her silk pajama set. She had pinned her hair up in a small twist, leaving wild strands of hair hanging down on the sides. Facing the large picture window, she could see all the lights

circling Lake Michigan. This is an enchant-
ing little place, she decided for the second
time that day. She was glad that Ray had
good taste. It was an important attribute in
a man—in *her* man.

Shutting her eyes, she cocked her head
back against the leather sofa. The music was
having a mesmerizing effect. She was being
hypnotized by the smooth sounds of Kim
Waters. The saxophone solo was just breaking through a vocal section when the stereo
volume suddenly increased. Georgette lifted
her head from the sofa and stared at the
stereo in confusion. Fumbling with the remote control, she decreased the volume until
the little red light had almost disappeared.
But the pitch was still getting higher.

Turning about-face to capture the tall
shadow looming over her, Georgette gasped
for air. She could feel shock waves penetrating through her body. Immobilized with
astonishment, she eyed Ray. Was she dreaming? No way, she thought, leaning back
against the sofa. Ray had the brass instrument pressed firmly to his lips. His cheeks
were fully expanded to accommodate his
breathing. His fingers rolled up, down, over,
and under all the small brass buttons. In
the candlelight she watched his eyes, relaxed
but focused. He played brilliantly. He was so
intense, the way he lifted up on his toes
with every peak and leaned backwards with

every valley. He glided closer to Georgette with each note, until he was standing directly in front of her.

After hitting the last note, he let the brass instrument dangle from around his neck. Georgette rose and, shaking her head in disbelief, patted the small beads of sweat from his forehead with an orange table napkin. Reaching over his head, she lifted the multicolored strap from around his neck. She wanted to have a closer look at the powerful piece of machinery. Helping her to remove the instrument from around his neck, he handed the long, sleek object to her. She said nothing, only caressed the saxophone gently, then handed it back.

Still speechless, she headed toward the bedroom and motioned for him to follow. Obeying, he carefully laid the brass instrument on the sofa. "Good night, Mr. Saxophone," he whispered. It was time for Ray to put someone else to bed.

Twenty-two

Rachel was happy to smell the food simmering in her parents' house as she walked in.

"Good morning," she said, inhaling the smell of fried fish, homemade biscuits, grits, and gravy.

"Well, good morning," her father replied, kissing her on the forehead as he walked out the front door.

"Where are you going, Daddy?"

"I'm going down to your uncle Jeff's house to help him with some painting. I'll see you later."

Walking toward the kitchen, Rachel greeted her mother, "Hi Mom," she said, kissing her on the cheek. "Where's Anthony?"

"He's in there watching some cartoons with Erica."

"How come they're getting the royal breakfast this morning?" Rachel teased.

"What are you talking about, Rachel? I did the same thing for all of my youngsters." Her mother smiled. Rachel knew her mother would fly to the moon just to make her grandchildren happy.

"How was the show?"

"Good. Ray was there," she said, grabbing a biscuit.

"Wash your hands, girl! So, did you guys speak?"

"He didn't see me. He was too wrapped up in some woman."

"Rachel, what is it you want from that boy? Are you still in love with him or something?"

Rachel didn't respond. She would rather keep her feelings to herself. She couldn't explain to anyone what was going through her mind, her heart, or her soul. Seeing her ex-husband, the one she had pushed away, cuddled up with another woman at the Luther concert, brought back all the old feelings.

Who was she, anyway? She was sure she had never seen her before. Perhaps she was from out of town or out of state. For some reason, she had to know.

After filling her stomach, Rachel beckoned Anthony to get his things. Whenever it was time to leave his grandparents' house he would throw a fit. "Come on Anthony, we gotta go. Kiss Mama goodbye."

"Don't want to go, Mommy. Please, can I stay?" he whined.

"Maybe we will come back later, okay?" she offered.

He poked out his lips and mumbled an "okay."

Rachel picked up Anthony, kissed Erica and her mother, and left.

"Mommy, I want to see Daddy," he moaned as she strapped the seat belt across the car seat.

"So do I," she said, starting the car. "So do I."

Gerard was going crazy. He had tried every number that the operator had given him and so far none of the phone numbers was the magical one. He had to let it go, at least until Georgette returned. He had to get ready for today's fraternity meeting. The topic of discussion for the meeting was "Living Single as a Black Man in America." The fraternity had wanted him to be the guest speaker, but he passed on the offer. He didn't know if he wanted to be single any longer.

Looking in the bathroom mirror, he saw a lonely, pitiful face. Who was that man? Some of his peers would think his life was ideal, working as a consultant at a large corporation, making over $100,000 a year, driving two of the most popular automobiles, dressing in the most expensive clothing, wearing the Cartier, Rolex, or Omega watches, dancing around town with the prettiest women, and living in the most popular part of town.

It was a dream, a vision that many people hoped for, prayed for, even died for. He was fortunate, blessed even, to have accomplished all of these things. How many people at the age of thirty-three had all of the things that he did? But then, how many people at his age had more than what he had? Ray, for instance had Georgette, the one thing he didn't have.

The beeping of the pager snapped Ray from his sleep. Glancing at the clock, he reached over Georgette and picked up the small black object. He kissed Georgette on the back of her neck, then jumped out of bed.

"What's wrong?" she asked, her eyes still clamped shut.

"It's the firehouse. They need me to come down to the station. It's an emergency," he said, throwing on his blue pants and blue shirt. "I'll call my brother and have him come over until I get back, all right?"

"Don't worry about me. I'll be fine, really," Georgette said, sitting up in bed. "Don't bother your brother."

"Are you sure?"

"Yes, I'm sure," she insisted.

He ran into the bathroom and splashed some water on his face and brushed his teeth. Then he stood in the doorway and looked at her. "I'll call you as soon as I can, so answer the phone, okay?"

"Are you sure about that? I mean about me answering the phone?" she asked him on her way to the bathroom.

"Yes, I'm sure. I don't have anything to hide," he said, bending over to tie up his steel-toed shoes.

"What are you doing?" he asked.

"Brushing my teeth," she gurgled from the bathroom.

"Come give me some sugar, baby, before I leave."

"I thought you had enough sugar last night," she teased, returning to place a wet kiss on his lips.

"Help yourself to anything. Here's my pager number," he said, writing the number down on a memo pad. He also left her the firehouse number and Maxine's number.

"This is where you can find Joe. Maxine is his girlfriend. More than likely, they will come by this afternoon, so don't worry."

"I'm a woman, I'm going to be all right," she said, hugging him. "Ray, please be careful. I wouldn't want anything to happen to you."

Opening the door, he turned back and looked at her. *She belongs here,* he thought.

"Georgette."

"Yes Ray," she replied softly.

"You've got my heart, so handle it with care," he said, closing the door behind him.

"Yeah, well, brotherman, you've got mine too," she said, walking back toward the bathroom.

After showering, getting dressed, and eating some breakfast, Georgette pulled the sheets off the bed. Searching for some clean linens, she looked in his closets. He had everything hung and folded so perfectly. From what she could tell, he was a basic kind of guy with just the bare essentials. Flipping through his hangers, she counted four suits: one blue, one olive green, one dark gray, and one tweed; five pairs of dress slacks, seven dress shirts, four button-down sweaters, six pullover sweaters, eight ties, four pairs of jeans, three sweat suits, three pairs of sneakers, five pairs of dress shoes, and three pairs of casual shoes.

She went to his top chest of drawers. He had about six sleeveless T-shirts and five short-sleeved undershirts. In the second drawer was an array of underwear in all colors and styles. She counted sixteen pairs. Some were high cut, some were basic trunks. In the third drawer she found five pairs of silk boxers and two sets of silk pajamas. In the fourth drawer were a combination of sweatshirts and T-shirts with varying logos. The last drawer, contained a veritable arsenal of socks, all kinds and colors. This drawer had to be his favorite, she thought. He had at least twenty-five pairs, fifteen of which were dress. The designs ranged from paisley to polka dots, stripes to plaid. Now she knew what *not* to get him for Christmas. She closed the drawers, being careful to make sure everything was in place. Still looking for some clean sheets, Georgette halted her search when she heard the doorbell.

The clock she walked past to answer the door read 2:00 P.M. Ray had been gone over two hours and time was flying by. Figuring that the small-framed woman standing outside was Joe's girlfriend, she opened the door with a smile.

"Maxine?" she questioned.

"No, Rachel. Where's Ray?" she asked. She sauntered inside with a young boy following close behind.

"He's not here. I'm sorry, what did you say your name was?"

"Rachel. And you?"

"I'm Georgette. Was he expecting you?"

"He's always expecting me, honey, I'm the mother of his child," Rachel answered bitingly.

"I see. In that case, please make yourself comfortable. I was just about to warm up some lunch. Would you like some?"

Rachel examined the woman closely. Who did this beautiful, overconfident sister think she was?

"No. We just ate. So, where is Ray?"

"He had to step out for a while, but I expect him later on. Do you want me to tell him to call you?"

"Are you trying to put me out?" Rachel grilled.

"Not at all. I'll get you something cool to drink. Feel free to sit." Georgette smiled as she headed toward the kitchen.

From what Rachel could tell, it appeared that they had had a very romantic evening. The candles were burned to the very core and the saxophone was sleeping on the sofa.

"Mommy, who's that?" Anthony asked.

"It's nobody you need to concern yourself about, baby."

Overhearing Rachel's remark, Georgette rolled her eyes. So this was Ray's ex-wife. She was glad she had the opportunity to check the woman out.

"Is he fighting a fire?" Rachel asked, joining Georgette in the kitchen.

Georgette turned around as cool as she could and took her time in replying. "I believe so, but like I said, if you need to talk to him you can wait here." She handed Rachel a glass of lemonade then slid past Rachel and moved to the dining area.

"Actually, I'm here to drop Anthony off. Did he tell you that?" Rachel asked testily.

"No, I can't say that he did," Georgette said, with a bright smile.

"I'm leaving now. Anthony has everything in his bag. Tell Ray I'll be back on Monday to pick him up," she said, snatching her purse off the table. Anthony had wandered over to his toy chest and was pulling out everything in sight.

"Anthony, come give Mommy a kiss goodbye," she directed.

"Where going Mommy?" Anthony asked.

"I'm going out of town," she said, eyeing Georgette. "But your daddy will be here soon, okay?"

"Okay," he said, kissing his mother before running back to his toy chest.

Georgette didn't say a word. Perhaps because she was caught off guard and she really didn't know how true any of this stuff was. Why was Rachel leaving Anthony with a stranger? Why didn't Ray tell her that he was expecting Anthony?

"Have my husband give me a call as soon as he steps his size tens in here, you hear?" Rachel demanded, slamming the door behind her.

Georgette was glad she was gone, but afraid of how Anthony might react once it sunk in that his mommy was gone and his daddy wasn't home. Deciding not to panic, Georgette carried on with her chores, peeking in on Anthony, who was engrossed in his toys, every so often. Georgette was preoccupied with how she might approach him.

Looking through the large entertainment center, she found a videotape of a Disney classic.

"Anthony, would you like to see *101 Dalmatians?*"

"Yeah! Yeah!" he squealed happily, running over to join her.

"Great! This will be fun!" Georgette popped the movie in and pressed the start button. Anthony wanted her to fast forward past the previews but she didn't want to fool too much with the remote. Moving the saxophone to the bedroom, she laid it on the unmade bed. She still had to find some sheets before Ray got home.

Ray couldn't believe his eyes. There was not a sound in the house but the static of the TV. Georgette and Anthony were sleeping on the sofa when Ray walked through the door. Georgette was sleeping on the outside of one end of the sofa while Anthony slept on the inside of the opposite end of the sofa.

He kneeled down beside Georgette. "Georgette," he whispered. "Georgette, wake up."

Springing up suddenly, Georgette looked over at Anthony first, then Ray.

"Hi," she said, rubbing her eyes. "When did you get in?"

"Just now. How did Anthony get here?"

"Your ex-wife dropped him off. She said you were expecting him."

"What? She just dropped him off and left?" Ray sounded angry.

"Something like that."

Ray yanked the phone out of the cradle and began pressing numbers furiously. As Rachel's answering machine picked up, Ray shouted into the phone, "I don't know what you're tripping on Rachel, but this time,you have gone too far. Call me when you get in." He slammed the phone down so hard it woke Anthony out of his sleep.

"Daddy, Daddy!" he said, sliding off the sofa.

"Hey, little man," Ray said, swooping Anthony up in his arms. Anthony gave Ray a kiss on the lips. "What were you watching?" he asked.

"One hundred one dematans!" Anthony shouted.

"Oh yeah? And who's that pretty lady you're watching it with?"

Anthony shrugged. "I don't know."

Ray and Georgette started laughing. Ray offered to take Anthony over to his mother's house but Georgette wouldn't hear of it. She was enjoying seeing Ray in his father role.

"I'm going to take a shower," Ray said. There were signs of soot and dirt on his face and hands. "Then we'll all go get something to eat and maybe go to the park or catch a movie, all right?" he asked.

"Okay, Daddy," Anthony agreed, bouncing around wildly. It was obvious that he adored his father.

"Sounds like a plan to me. Let's go see that dinosaur movie?" she said.

Ray smiled and said, "Anything you want, baby. The day is still yours."

Ray kept Anthony until Sunday afternoon, then took the boy over to Rachel's parents, since Rachel herself had not returned his calls. His mother-in-law, Liz, answered the door after the third ring.

"Ray? Well, what a surprise. Come on in. How's my baby doing?" she said, picking Anthony up and kissing him on the cheek. Anthony motioned to his grandmother that he wanted to get down. As soon as she released him, he ran inside the house calling for "Pop-Pop."

"Sorry to drop by unexpectedly but I had no other choice. Rachel dropped Anthony off at my house yesterday out of the blue. I have an out-of-town trip planned for the remainder of the weekend. I tried calling her, but she hasn't responded to my calls. The only thing I could think of was to bring Anthony over here."

"That's fine, Ray. You know we are always happy to spend some time with Anthony. Don't worry about a thing. You say

Rachel hasn't returned your calls? I hope everything is okay."

Ray didn't dare share his thoughts about Rachel. He was sure the only thing wrong with Rachel was her bruised ego. Not wanting to waste any more time, he thanked his ex-mother-in-law, said goodbye to Anthony, and headed for the door. He wanted to get home. Georgette was waiting for him there.

"Thanks again for taking Anthony. Tell Rachel I'll speak with her on Tuesday when I pick him up."

"Don't mention it. And Ray, don't be a stranger," she said, smiling.

He wanted to make sure that he could devote the rest of the weekend entirely to Georgette. He felt a little guilty about leaving Anthony, but he figured he would pick the boy up the day after tomorrow. That's when he would find out what kind of a stunt Rachel was trying to pull.

Parking the car in the short-term parking lot, Ray quietly unloaded her bags from the back of the Explorer. Holding Georgette's hand, they walked toward the terminal.

"I had a great time," she said, facing him.

"I'm happy to hear that. I hope that we will have many more times like this," he said seriously.

"I hope so, too. Are you coming to visit me next month?"

"Consider it a done deal. I'll pick up my tickets next week."

"Good. I'll plan a fun-filled weekend for us on the East Coast." She smiled.

Ray embraced her, then gave her a long, lingering kiss.

"Georgette, I'm falling hard, baby. Are you sure you want that to happen?"

She smiled and pulled him closer. "Don't worry about it. I'll catch you if I have to." She left her ruby mark on his lips as she pulled out of his grasp. "I'll call you when I get in. And Ray, you may need to catch me too." She smiled one last time before turning to board the plane.

Twenty-three

"So what did you say?"

"I told him yes, of course. Georgette, you will not believe it. Don and I were in the kitchen fixing dinner when out of nowhere he tells me to go sit down because I'm in the way. So I did. He finished making dinner, then called me to the table. I admit I was a little irritated about being kicked out of the kitchen but I figure, what the hell, I could use the rest. Anyway, we sit down, say grace, and start eating. The TV's blaring in the background, all the lights are on, everything just seemed normal. Then he asked me if I wanted some wine with dinner. I'm thinking, what's the occasion? And of course, me being the lush I am, told him yes. He gave me some line about the wine not being chilled and that he would drop a few ice cubes in the glass. Georgette, I'm telling you, I had no clue what was up. Except when I lifted my glass up to my mouth, I noticed something sparkling that was like no ice cube I had ever seen. I pulled the glass closer to my eyes so that I could inspect the object further. And *bam!* There was this incredible engagement ring floating in the glass. Girl, I about hit the floor. He started grinning and then popped the famous question: *Will you marry me?* I said yes faster than your next heartbeat."

"Oh my God! How romantic, Melinda. I'm so happy for you!" Georgette said, fighting back the tears. "Did you guys set a date yet?"

"How does Labor Day weekend sound to you?"

"I'll be there come rain or shine."

"Maybe Ray will be able to come out for the weekend?"

"Possibly. We'll just have to wait and see. I still can't believe it, Melinda, you're finally moving to Philly! After all these years of begging and pleading with you, Don managed to talk you into it."

"I know, can you believe it? I'm marrying the man I should have married in the first place. Georgette, I am so happy I could scream."

"Then do it! Let it out, yell to the top of your lungs if you have to."

Melinda laughed. "How was your stay in Chicago?"

"It was wonderful, girl." Georgette briefly filled Melinda in on her romantic weekend with Ray. She told her about the candlelight dinner, the rose petals in the bathtub, the surprise Luther concert, and Ray's saxophone serenade. She even told her about the ex-Mrs. Fuschée.

"Wow! Sounds like Ray is trying hard to reel you in. What do you think about him, does he stand a chance?" Melinda asked.

"I think he just might," Georgette said as the intercom on her phone buzzed.

"Melinda, I've got another call coming in. I'll call you later tonight. Congratulations again."

Georgette hung up just as Anne's voice came through the speaker. "Gerard is on the line for you. He says it's urgent. What do you want me to do?" she asked.

"Tell him I'm in a meeting. Tell him I haven't made it in yet. Tell him anything you want, Anne."

Georgette had no intention of speaking to Gerard now. She was still riding high on the euphoria of her weekend and the way Ray had treated her like a queen. The way he'd rubbed her back, the way he'd poured his love into every moment he'd spent with her. It was a wonderful feeling, so why in heaven's name would she want to ruin everything by talking to Gerard Jenkins?

Gerard was calling Georgette daily. It was getting to the point where she had to screen her calls at home and park her car in her neighbor's garage. At first, she was flattered by the attention. But now she was becoming concerned. Gerard was acting like some kind of possessed spirit, haunting her. She entertained the idea of changing her phone number, but she knew that Gerard would eventually be able to access it. Gerard was well connected; he had sources in every line of business imaginable.

She was happy that Melinda was in town for the weekend. They planned to do some shopping for a wedding dress and attend to some other things in preparation for the happy event.

She heard the phone ringing as she stepped into the shower. It was probably Melinda, she thought, calling to wake her up. Drying her hands off before picking up the phone, she cleared her throat. "It's the early bird that catches the man," she said.

"That's cute, Georgette. Are you ready?" Melinda queried.

"Almost. I need to jump in the shower real quick and then I'm good to go."

"You'll never believe where I'm calling you from."

"Where? Don?" she laughed.

"Why is your mind always in the toilet? I'm outside your door."

"For real?"

"Yeah, for real, so come open up the door

and don't hug me or kiss me till you brush your teeth," her friend joked.

"Shut up, Melinda," Georgette teased, peeping through the blinds. "I'll unlock the front door for you. Meanwhile, I'm going to get wet."

Melinda made her way up the stairs to the front door. Giving the living room a quick once-over, she dropped her purse and keys on the sofa. Wanting something cold to quench her thirst, Melinda strolled into the kitchen, observing the new plants and paintings Georgette had acquired since her last visit. Her friend would spit fire if she saw her reach into the refrigerator without washing her hands first, Melinda thought, snatching a Pepsi off the shelf.

Melinda walked back into the living room. Stopping at the entertainment center, she began flipping through Georgette's CD collection. Their taste in music was one of the many things they had in common. After shuffling through the hundred or so CDs, Melinda picked up some pictures off the brass coffee table. Halfway through the batch, she heard Georgette opening the bathroom door.

"Hey, girl!" Georgette shouted, running over to greet her friend.

"Your teeth clean?" Melinda grinned, giving Georgette a hug. "You've lost some weight, Georgette. It looks good. Matter of fact, you look great!" Melinda circled her friend. "Have you been working out that hard?"

"Three, sometimes four times a week. I've slacked off since I got back from Chicago, but I'll pick it up again this week."

"Ray must have been knocked off his feet." Melinda smiled.

"He seems to like me in any way," Georgette replied with a wink.

"What you planning to do when he gets in town?" Melinda asked.

"I'm not sure yet. You know me, I'll plan something exciting. Maybe we'll drive up to Atlantic City with my brother Kyle and his girl Lisa. Or we could catch the train down to D.C. so Dorian and Phillip can meet him."

"Really? You going to chance having Dorian and Phillip psychoanalyze Ray?"

"Like I said, I'll figure it out before he gets here. Are you ready?"

"All set. I can't wait to become Mrs. Don Tolliver."

Georgette insisted that she drive her car so that it wouldn't be there if Gerard stopped by. She didn't want him thinking she was home; she wouldn't put it past him to camp out on her porch, thinking she'd eventually come outside.

"You mean to tell me he is still bothering you? Why don't you have Ray pay him a visit when he gets here? Or have him answer your phone for the weekend," Melinda advised.

"Now, that might be an idea. Maybe then he'll catch the drift. It could backfire though and send some sparks flying."

"So what! Ray's a firefighter. Have him put the sparks out."

"Can I ask you something?"

"Sure, after you make this light," directed Melinda.

"Let me handle the driving, okay? Anyway, why do you hate Gerard so much?"

"Georgette, I don't hate Gerard. I detest him. Look, I tried real hard when you two were together to give him the benefit of the doubt. I truly did. But I didn't like the way he treated you. The other women, the fact that he was always standing you up, placing his fraternity brothers before you. In addition to the fact that he once called me a charcoal mama. I've just never been able to get past that."

Georgette didn't respond. Perhaps because she knew that Melinda was right about everything. The only thing Melinda forgot to give him credit for was his apparent love for her. No matter how many women or how many broken dates, Gerard always managed to find his way home, back into her arms and back into her life.

Traffic was thick as they pulled into the mall parking lot. People were out in numbers, walking to and from the shoppers' paradise.

"Georgette, look! That looks like Cheryl Gray over there by that car. Drive over there!"

"It's her all right. Look at her, she's showing already." Georgette could feel her heart sinking at the thought that it was Gerard's baby she was carrying.

"Drive over there so I can get a look at her."

"What am I supposed to do, Melinda? I've got all these cars in front of me."

"Pull over here! Never mind, I'll be right back."

Melinda was out the car door before Georgette could say another word.

"Damn," Georgette mumbled. What was Melinda up to with this pregnant girl? Her eyes followed Melinda's strides. Cheryl quickened her actions when she saw the other woman approach.

"Well, if it isn't Cheryl Gray," Melinda said in a sarcastic tone.

"What do you want, Melinda?" Cheryl frowned.

"Nothing much. So, when are you due?"

"Why? What's it to you?" Cheryl said, opening her car door.

Melinda abruptly choked off her thoughts of wanting to strangle Cheryl. Instead she simply stared at the woman for a few seconds, shook her head, turned, and walked back toward Georgette. Why bother? she thought. They were all getting too old for this nonsense. "Life is too short," she murmured, smiling to herself.

"What did you say to her Melinda?" Georgette asked, getting out of the parked car.

"Nothing, really. I was tempted to spit out some truly belligerent things, I must confess, but then I caught myself."

"That's wiser, girlfriend. Nothing's going to change what happened, you know? Let's go, we have a lot of ground to cover here." Georgette started out toward the Bloomingdales outlet.

Cheryl watched Melinda until she was out of sight. She knew that Georgette was probably somewhere nearby. With that in mind, she hurried into her car before her foes had an opportunity to strike again. She could feel the tears welling up in her eyes as she exited the parking lot. What had she done to deserve all of these ill feelings directed toward her? Why was everyone out to get her? She refused to raise her baby in such a hostile environment. She was going to have to talk to Gerard and sort things out. To begin with, she wanted to know what kind of a role Gerard was planning to play in the upbringing of their child. Then, she would figure out a city or state that she could escape to in order to get a fresh start. She could put in for a transfer to Cincinnati. She had lots of relatives there, and she loved the area. "First things first," she murmured. She would speak with Gerard and try one more time to change his mind about her and the baby.

With all the walking they had done in the heat that day, all Georgette could think about was a cool shower. No one could easily contend with the heat during the summer in Philadelphia. The moment she stepped out of the shower, she heard the ringing of the phone. Racing to answer it like her life depended on it, she snatched it up before her machine picked up.

"Hello," she panted.

"Hi, baby, what you doing?"

"Ray! How are you, sweetheart?"

"I'm doing bunches better now that I'm talking to you," he said affectionately.

"I'm glad to hear that. I just got out of the shower twenty seconds ago."

"I know. That's why I called," he said seductively.

"Stop it, Ray. We both know we can't continue with this line of talk over the phone. So how's Mr. Saxophone? Have you been working on some new material?"

"We sure have. In fact, I'll bring him with me when I come there so you can hear it firsthand. How about that?"

"Sounds good to me. So, what else is going on with you? How's Anthony?"

There was a brief pause as Georgette's call-waiting line clicked. "Hold on a minute, Ray, okay?"

Clicking over to the incoming call, she knew she was taking a chance that the person on the other line could be Gerard. And as soon as she said hello, she knew beyond a reasonable doubt that it was her old flame just by the way he breathed.

"Gerard, I'm on the other line. It's long distance."

"Georgette, I need to see you. Can I please stop by for just a few minutes?"

"No way, Gerard. Why do you continue to call? What do you want from me?"

"Like I told you before, I want, I desire, I hope for one more chance, a chance for you and me. I love you, Georgette. I've never stopped loving you, through everything. I will never stop trying or caring for you. I'm ready now for us to be together forever, for the rest of our lives. I swear before God, Georgette, if you would just grant me this one last opportunity, I will never, ever hurt your precious heart again. Please let me come over so we can talk. Please?"

"I'm sorry, Gerard, but I don't believe your promises any longer. I just can't do it. I won't do it! I've got to go, there's another call."

"Is it what's-his-name?"

"Bye, Gerard."

"Wait, wait! All right, I understand. But could you do one last thing for me?"

She heard the phone line click. Ray had hung up. "What, Gerard? I've got to go."

"Would you meet me for dinner one day next week?"

"No!"

"Please, just one more dinner and then I'll be out of your hair. I have to fly to Chicago and close the deal with EPI and First Bank of Chicago. So how about it? Lunch or dinner next Thursday or Friday?"

She took a deep breath, then let it out slowly. What was she about to do? Hadn't she been through enough torture? But she couldn't seem to hold up under his persistence. It was like he was destined to redeem himself. Never before in their entire five-year history had he begged and pleaded so much. She almost felt sorry for him. Almost. All she knew was that even after all the pain, anger, humiliation, and turmoil, she couldn't bring herself to hate him.

She had to let her feelings for Gerard go at some point, though, if she wanted to be truly free for Ray. She would have to put this chapter behind her and soon. Perhaps it would do her some good to see him, perhaps it was what she needed, to put some closure on the past. Shaking her head in disbelief, she formed the words, "All right, Gerard. Let's meet next Friday. I'll meet you at Jeremy's after work. Don't be late."

"Thank you, Georgette, thank you. I'll see you then. I love you."

Just like that, the words flowed from his

lips so easily. What in God's name was she doing? she thought.

Looking at the clock, she realized that fifteen minutes had elapsed since the time she put Ray on hold. She was flooded with guilt. Pressing the reset button, she dialed Ray's number and waited.

"Hello?" he answered softly.

"Ray, I'm so sorry about that. I hope you're not upset with me."

Naturally he was upset, livid, in fact. He couldn't place his finger on it, but he knew something was wrong. Maybe he would feel better when she explained the situation to him. He wanted to know who that person was on the other line and why it had taken her so long to call him back. He could gather from her tone of voice that it hadn't been an emergency.

"It's okay, Georgette. Was something wrong?" He tried to keep his voice even.

"Oh no, nothing like that. So anyway, where were we? Oh yeah, finish telling me about Anthony."

Ray couldn't help but feel irritated that she had chosen not to explain to him about the phone call. She must have her reasons, he decided.

"Never mind Anthony. So what about lover boy? Has he attempted a comeback?" he asked, unable to mask his jealousy.

Shucks! she thought. She didn't want to get

into a conversation with Ray about Gerard. Especially since she had just hung up with him. The cards had been dealt to her and she didn't know what hand to play.

"Kind of," she said finally. "He's trying to repair the damage he's done, I guess."

"Really? Did he call just recently or a while ago?"

"He's been calling for a while now," she said softly.

"Do you think he has a chance?" Ray asked softly.

Do monkeys have a tail? This was Gerard he was asking about, after all. The comeback kid himself.

"I've been through too much Ray. There's no way he could ever restore my trust. Too much has been irreparably destroyed. Take your cousin, for instance. She's just one piece of the puzzle. By the way, have you spoken to her recently?"

"Not recently. I left her a message telling her that I would be in town the weekend after next and that I would hang out with her for a day once I got there."

Georgette didn't say a word. She felt the irritation building. Why was he bothering to spend his money to come to Philly if he wasn't planning to spend the entire weekend with her, not the woman who would like nothing better than to destroy all Georgette held dear? The writing on the wall was clearer than the finest diamond on the earth. His cousin would be in their lives forever. That's if Georgette chose to be a part of Ray's life for that long. She was talking herself into a fury now. What she really wanted to do was hang up. Gerard, Cheryl and now Ray were starting to madden her beyond belief.

"Georgette, I want to make something very clear to you," Ray said, cutting through the sudden tense silence. "I adore you. Hell, to be very direct, I love you. I've never loved a woman the way I've grown to love you. I feel like someone kidnapped me one night, dipped me in a vat filled with Georgette tonic, and set me loose. My love for you is consuming. Do you hear what I'm saying to you? You are the woman I wish I had taken my vows with the first time. You should have been my wife and the mother of my child."

Georgette was spellbound. Vows? Wife? *Oh my God*, she said to herself, *this sounds like a proposal.*

"I want you to be my wife," he continued. "I pray every night that God grants me that one desire of my heart. I can't even put into words this feeling I have about you. All I know is that I think about you every day. You are a fine woman, Georgette. Not just externally but internally as well. You have morals, standards that I admire and believe in. I love the way you communicate, I love your honesty. I love your flexibility, your realistic expectations. The way you handled my ex-wife dropping Anthony off at the house was truly gracious. Your interaction with my son was caring, natural. There are so many qualities I admire in you, I could go on all night. Let me put it to you this way. I've sunk, Georgette, so deep that there is no turning back for me, not now, not tomorrow, not ever. If this is too much for you to handle, or if you don't feel it too, then now is the time to tell me."

The anger that Georgette had felt instantly vanished. "Ray, where have you been all of my life? This is not too much for me to handle and no, I don't want out. I will admit that I have to be cautious. It's only natural considering all that has gone on with us. What about the long distance between us? We can't maintain a relationship this way for much longer."

"Is that your only concern? Are there any other worries?"

"Just one. Your cousin. How are you going to handle that?"

"Listen to me closely, Georgette. First of all, I don't have a problem relocating to Philadelphia, or relocating you to Chicago if that is what it will take for us to be together. Secondly, with regards to Lynn, I love my cousin very much. But if I had to make a decision, it would be for you to be the next and last Mrs. Ray Fuschée. Like I said before, I'm in it all the way, baby. I'm yours and you have my heart, just be respectful of it, that's all I ask."

"Mrs. Ray Fuschée huh? I might be able to handle that," she said, barely able to contain her excitement.

Hanging the phone up, Georgette stood staring into the large mirror attached to her closet. Plopping down on the bed, she reached over to the wicker magazine rack next to the nightstand. She pulled out an old issue of *Brides* magazine. *Here we go again,* she thought.

In the week to come Georgette underwent attacks of anxiety. She couldn't believe that she had agreed to meet Gerard after work. More surprisingly, she couldn't believe how secretive she was being about the meeting. She was sure Anne suspected something, but her secretary never did confront her about it. She felt guilty about hiding the news from Melinda. But she also didn't want to be lectured. What if Ray found out? What would happen then? She had to be extra careful not to been seen with Gerard. Especially with Cheryl around.

She sucked in a deep breath, then released it as she entered the lobby at Jeremy's. The after-work crowd was spilling in. She had selected Jeremy's because it was located on the opposite side of town. She was hoping that no one who knew her or Gerard would be there. She noticed Gerard sitting at a window booth. A long white box was on the table in front of him. It was probably a dozen long-stemmed roses, she thought.

Gerard stood up to greet her as she walked over to the table.

"Georgette, you're looking incredible. You've lost weight, I see. Please, have a seat," he motioned her into the booth, then slid in close beside her.

"Thank you," she said, looking him over. He looked handsome as ever. Like he had just stepped out of a men's magazine.

"Thank you for meeting me, I really appreciate it. Here, this is for you," he said, handing her the box.

The box felt surprisingly light as she began opening it. Tipping her head further into the box, she took out a smaller package. Glancing at Gerard with a puzzled expression, she carefully unwrapped the small item. Her mouth fell open as she fingered the diamond and ruby bracelet inside.

"Gerard, this is beautiful, but I can't accept it."

"Why not? Look, Georgette, I don't want you to think I'm trying to buy my way back into your life, but I had to show you how much you still mean to me. I'm sure you know that generosity has never been a problem for me. I have my faults, I admit, but showing you how much I love you has never been one of them. Please keep this as a token of my undying love for you. The heart represents our hearts. The ruby represents my blood and the strength of my love for you; the diamonds surrounding the heart are symbolic as well. They represent your tears for the pain I've caused you, which have now crystallized into a fortress around your heart. I love you so much, Georgette Willis. I don't want to ever wake up without you by my side. Please, just give me another chance. Tell me what I need to do and I swear I will do it."

Georgette focused silently on the bracelet. From everything Gerard had said, the trinket was a symbol of his love, of their love. She looked into his eyes, and knew that his soul was laid bare; it was as clear as the tears that were starting to form in the corners of his eyes. There was no doubt in her heart that this time he was sincere. *Damn you, Gerard,* she thought. *Why now, after all this time, all these years? Why have you come to this realization now?* If he hadn't suspected she had a new man in her life, would he have come around? She picked up the bracelet and gave it back to him.

"I don't think it will fit," she said.

"It will fit, Georgette, I know it will," he said, unfastening the clasp and placing it on her right wrist.

She stared at her wrist for a long moment,

feeling herself weaken. "It's beautiful Gerard. Thank you."

What had happened to her resolve? The jazz band was filling the room with nostalgic songs such as "My Funny Valentine," "Mood Indigo," and "Stormy Weather." Gerard had ordered her lobster in wine sauce, and the waiter was popping the cork on a bottle of Dom Perignon. What to do now? she thought. The night was still much too young.

Twenty-four

Georgette, feeling no pain from the Dom Perignon, plopped down on the sofa.

"Thanks, Gerard, for driving me home. I shouldn't have finished that last glass. How are you feeling?"

"I'm fine. You know I could always hold my alcohol better than you, remember?"

"Yeah, I remember. But there were a whole lot of things you couldn't hold at all, if you get my drift."

"I realize that now. Let me get you a sheet or something to lay over you. Will you be all right?"

"Sure I will. I can make it to my room," she said, standing up to walk. Gerard caught her as she stumbled on the coffee table.

"Let me help you," he said.

"Don't try any funny stuff, Gerard. I'm not in the mood for it."

Gerard smiled to himself. He had never seen her so tipsy before. Perhaps Mr. Fuschée couldn't afford good champagne, he thought.

Sliding off her shoes, he propped her head

against the large pillows. Cradling her feet between his hands, he began massaging them.

"Gerard, don't do that," she said pleadingly.

"Don't worry, Georgette, I'm not going to take advantage of you in your condition. Just relax and let me smooth away the tension, all right?" From the sighing she was doing he knew she was enjoying it. She always enjoyed his foot massages. He could feel the tightness of his underwear pinching as he watched her lovely face softening. Her hand fell over her stomach and he watched her breasts rise and fall with each breath.

Before long Georgette was sleeping and Gerard was content just to be in her presence.

He kicked off his shoes, kissed her forehead, and turned off the lights. "Good night, sweetheart," he whispered. "It feels good to be back."

Georgette woke up in the middle of the night feeling hot and crowded. As she lifted her head from the body invading her space, she felt a sharp pain run through her head. At first, she couldn't make out the person lying next to her. *Who is that?* she wondered. But after blinking her eyes and shaking her head a few times, her vision focused and her mind acknowledged—Gerard. *Oh God,* she thought, easing out of bed. *What have I done?*

Tracing her hand along the wall, she fumbled into the bathroom. Flipping on the light,

she looked into the mirror. What she saw was
a woman with mascara circling the bottom of
her eyelids and lipstick smeared above her up-
per lip.

"Oh God," she groaned. She felt like she
had drunk four bottles of liquor and then
jumped on the fastest roller coaster on earth.
The events of the evening came back to her.
Thank God things hadn't gone too far, she
thought.

She attempted to wash her face. Drying
off, she looked in the mirror once more. She
noticed the reflection of the diamonds hanging from her wrist. Glimpsing down at the
bracelet, she examined it with her left hand.
It was the most extraordinary piece of jewelry she had ever seen. She headed back to
the bedroom.

Gerard had shifted positions. He was lying
on his side now, but he wasn't asleep. Georgette slid back into bed as Gerard turned to
face her.

"Are you okay?" he asked.

"Just fine, thanks," she said, slipping her
head under his arms.

"Georgette, I love you so much," he whispered, pulling her closer.

"Gerard, I don't know about all this. I
think . . ." She attempted to continue, but
Gerard had seized her mouth with his lips
and was entwining her tongue with his

tongue. "Marry me, Georgette." He blew into her ear as he started kissing her neck.

"Gerard, don't," she begged. "I'm not ready for this."

He sighed and went still. "I understand," he whispered, rolling onto his back. "Do you mind if I just hold you in my arms?"

"No, I suppose I wouldn't mind that," she whispered, laying her head on his chest. Her head still swam. All she wanted to do was sleep. "Good night, Gerard."

"Good night, Georgette," he said, kissing her on the forehead.

Gerard lay awake, staring at the ceiling. His mind was zooming in a trillion directions as he replayed the evening over in his head. Holding Georgette in his arms all night could be measured as a great step toward realizing his vision to have her back in his life. *Yup, I'm on the road again.* He smiled, drifting off into a deep slumber.

For the next week, Georgette was a different person. She didn't know how to deal with her feelings. Maybe this is how amnesia victims felt when they get their memory back, she thought. She was happy that Gerard had gone to Chicago for a few weeks. He had phoned her nearly every day to proclaim his love for her. Apparently, he mistook their evening together as a sure sign of reconciliation.

She was sure that Ray had detected the

change in her. She was mulling the situation over in her mind one day at work when Anne interrupted her thoughts. "Georgette, Gerard is holding for you."

"Thanks, Anne," she said, picking up the telephone.

"Hi, Gerard."

"Hello, Georgette. How's my girl doing today?"

"Your girl?"

"Yeah, my girl. Why, are you having second thoughts?" he asked.

"Gerard, we need to talk when you get back."

"Talk? I can think of something better we can do. How about you pick me up from the airport Friday and we go directly to the chapel and get married?"

"Married? Gerard, please, I've got plans for Friday night." *What, is he nuts? More than likely, this is another one of his win-Georgette-over stunts. And even if he is sincere, Ray is coming into town Friday,* she thought.

"That's fine, Georgette," he said. "Tell you what, I'll try and catch an earlier flight home. Once I get there, we'll make a quick detour and then you can go on with your plans for the evening as Mrs. Gerard Jenkins. How's that sound?"

Startled, she didn't respond. She had been offered a proposal of sorts by Ray just last week. Who would have thought it possible?

Two men, two loves, and two marriage proposals all within two weeks. What would she do now?

Hanging the phone up, she swiveled around in her chair. She stared out the office window, immersing herself in the bustle of the city. She affixed her attention on the rushing yellow cabs, the steam rising from the manholes, the people hustling across the streets, the haste of the other drivers, and the expert pedaling of the bicycle delivery people. She could feel a connection between the madness outside her window and the turmoil within her soul. What, how, why her? She had read about this type of thing happening, but never imagined that it would be happening to *her*. She had two days to figure things out, today and tomorrow. Wanting desperately to call Melinda for advice, she intercepted herself. This dilemma was one that she had to find a solution to all by herself.

Georgette was home doing some light dusting when the cordless phone rang.

"Hello?" she answered, sitting down on the bed.

"Georgette, this is Ray. Is everything all right with you?"

"Of course. Why do you ask?"

"I don't know, you seem distracted these last few weeks. Have I done something to upset you?"

"No, not at all. I guess I'm just feeling some stress on the job," she lied. She wasn't ready to tell Ray about Gerard, especially not over the phone. They would have an opportunity to discuss things once he got in tomorrow night.

"So, do you have an action-packed weekend planned for us?"

"Of course! First, I thought we would start out by taking a drive to Atlantic City Saturday afternoon. Kyle and his girlfriend are going to meet us there. Then, we could ride down to Virginia to see my sister and her husband."

"Sounds good to me. Do you think your family will approve of me?"

What kind of question is that, she thought. Who cares whether or not her family likes him. She had greater issues at hand to deal with. Mainly, what to do about him and Gerard this weekend. Knowing Gerard, he would stop by unannounced with some flowers and a ring. What a scene that would be. The only way to avoid the potential chaos would be to keep Ray on the road all weekend. Even with all of the emotions surfacing with Gerard, she was excited about seeing Ray again.

"I think they will love you," she declared.

"Good, because there is nothing worse than having your future in-laws despise you. Say, do you have a grill so we can barbecue?"

"I sure don't. You know, my brother asked

me the same thing the other day. What is it with you men? Is that the only thing you can cook on?"

"Now, come on, Georgette, you of all people should know better." Ray laughed. "My, my, my, how quickly we forget."

"Oh, no, my memory hasn't failed me. I remember the seafood specialty that you whipped up for me. Or rather, that your mom whipped up for you and that you warmed up for me," she teased.

"Oh, okay," he said. "See if I cook for you again." He chuckled. "Anyway, I better go. I've still got some packing to do. I'm looking forward to seeing you tomorrow. I hope you're as excited as I am. Have them lips softened up, you hear?"

Georgette hesitated only a moment. "Why certainly, sweetheart. I can't wait to see you either."

After speaking with Ray, she could feel her heartbeat pumping with excitement. Reminiscing about her weekend in Chicago, she stumbled upon something. Her feelings for Ray were real and solid. *My God*, she thought, *is it possible to love two men at once?*

Twenty-five

"I don't know what to do, Melinda. Ray is such a sweet brother. He's the ideal man. The kind women hope and pray for. I feel completely comfortable and open with him. I can be myself all the time. Actually, he's the only man on this earth who doesn't seem to mind me going to bed with a silk scarf wrapped around my head. You know what I mean? With Gerard, I always have to be concerned about the image thing, my looks, how I'm dressed, if my nails are done, what I say, and so on and so on."

"Who you telling? That's what made me take a second hard look at Don. When I was with Greg, I felt like I had to be on stage all the damn time. If I had a cracked nail, a hair out of place, or, God forbid, a mask on my face, he would fart a watermelon. I can't believe how silly I was acting. I would rush home every day, take a shower, comb my hair, start dinner, and then change my clothes so that I could be nice and fresh before he arrived home. It was my own fault and I have no one to blame but myself. But now, I don't have to be preoccupied with that trivial stuff. All I have to do is to continue with whatever it was that made Don happy to be with me in the first place. And that, my dear friend, is to simply be me. But anyway, what exactly are you saying? Do you love Ray enough to marry him? Or is Gerard cock-blocking again?"

"Come on, Melinda, you're comparing kiwis to bananas. They both have a place in my heart. They both have put their best efforts forward these past few weeks. The difference is, one is definitely better for me than the other, but I have a history with one that I cannot deny. Gerard swears on his daddy's grave that he's changed and I can't help but want to believe him."

"This is so exciting," giggled Melinda. "What are you going to do, Georgette? Who will be the fortunate man to win your love?"

"I have no idea what I'm going to do."

"If you ask me, I think you should take some time away from them both and get some perspective on the situation. Someone is going to get hurt, that's a definite. Especially since neither one of them has a clue that the other has proposed to you. Girl, just take your time and sit back and relax. What's the rush, anyhow? Enjoy the attention for a while. Do you take man number one or man number two? Who knows, maybe you'll be able to trade them both in for the man behind door number three." Melinda laughed.

"Door number three? That would be way too much for me to handle."

"Georgette, nothing is too much for you to handle. Please remember that, all right? Anyway, we better get off the phone. Don't you need to earn your paycheck today?"

"Sure do. I'll give you a call later. I'm going to leave a little early today. I have some errands to do before my men get in," Georgette sighed, hanging up the phone.

Stretching her arms above her head, she focused on the small ivy plant sitting on her desk. This was going to be a "fill in the blanks" type of weekend, she thought.

Georgette's first step was food shopping after she left work. She grabbed a cart outside of the grocery store and set her mind to the task at hand.

She had to put a quick glide in her stride if she was going to complete everything before Ray arrived. Happy that she had already picked up the movies from the video store, she sped past the video section. Reaching the seafood counter, she peered under the glass top. She would get a pound of shrimp, a pound of scallops, and a half pound of fresh blue crab meat. Unconsciously, she licked her lips as the clerk filled her order.

After loading up the trunk with groceries, she swung by the florist. Flowers were definitely needed to set off her table decor. Deciding that Ray was deserving of some special treatment, she purchased a dozen roses. She wondered if he had ever received flowers from a woman before. He would tonight.

She then set off for the cleaners. She decreased the volume on her stereo as she pulled into the parking lot. Bill didn't like to hear his customers arriving from a block away. It had been ages since she had done business with the little dry cleaning shop. Probably because of the thing with her and Gerard. After all, Gerard had been the one to introduce her to the owner of the small but reliable shop. Bill greeted her warmly when she walked through the door. "Here comes my favorite person in all of Philadelphia. How you doing today, Georgette?" he asked.

"Fine, Bill, how are you?"

"I'm hanging in there for an old man," he said, turning toward the rotary machine. "Here we go, Ms. Lady. You've got a big load today, huh? What, you going out of town again without inviting me?" He laughed.

"Bill, you're so sweet." She smiled, digging in her purse to find her wallet.

"How's that mutual friend of ours? You seen him lately?" he asked.

She knew he was referring to Gerard. But she could also sense he was fishing for information. From the first time she met him,

Bill had been one of her and Gerard's top supporters. She knew he wanted desperately for things to work out between the two of them.

Tugging a twenty from inside her wallet, she replied, "He's all right I suppose. Haven't you seen him?"

"I ain't seen that boy for weeks. Matter of fact, if he don't get in here and pick up these clothes soon, I'm going to start charging him storage!"

"He's been out of town, but I'm sure he'll be in tomorrow. Monday at the latest."

"Out of town? Where he go to now?"

"Chicago. He's finishing up some big deal there. I'm sure you'll hear all about it," she said, straining to pick up the large bundle. The plastic covering on the clothes made it hard for her to handle them without mashing them together.

"Here, let me give you a hand with this," Bill said, lifting up the counter top so that he could assist her. "I'll sure be glad when you and that there boy get married so he can carry your clothes. So, how are things with the two of you? I told him to go on and hitch you before someone else does."

Now was as good a time as any to plant a bug in Bill's ear about Ray and his proposal. For some reason, she wanted the news to travel back to Gerard. Bill was just the right person to get the job done. Bracing herself, she formulated the sounds that finally produced the sentence. "To be honest with you, Bill, someone else *has* already proposed to me."

The look of surprise on his face made her feel ashamed of herself. He was obviously distressed about her news.

"Say what? Somebody like who? Not that boy whose cousin is knocked up with Gerard's child."

She couldn't believe her ears. Gerard must have been feeding him information about everything all along. How could he do that? Determined to keep her ground, she replied, "Yeah, that's the one."

"You're fooling me. Did you accept the proposal?"

"Not yet, I'm still trying to resolve some things. I'm sure after this weekend, things will be a lot clearer to me," she said.

"He's in town?"

"In a few hours he will be. In fact, I better put a step on it. I still have to get some gas and go by the car wash."

"Don't let me hold you up then. Take your time before you make a decision, you hear me? Be sure now, 'cause it ain't no fun doing it a second time. Understand, sugar?" He kissed her on the cheek. "Take your time," he reiterated, walking back toward the counter. "You've got all your life to be somebody's wife. Or, second wife in his case."

A wise man, Georgette thought as she left the shop. He was right, she did have her entire life to become somebody's wife. Why had she been feeling so pressured to lose her identity in the first place? Furthermore, she loved her name. Georgette Willis was what she knew best. How was she going to relate to Georgette Fuschée or Georgette Jenkins, anyhow? "Whatever," she sighed. She didn't have all night to think about this. She had to hurry home to get dinner prepared. But first, she had two more stops to make, one to the gas station and one to the car wash.

Twenty-six

Ray, throwing his bags into the lobby, slammed the door behind him. He could hear the phone ringing as he placed the key in the lock, but it was too late. He was packed and ready to trade in the Windy City for a cheesesteak weekend in Philly.

After parking in the long-term lot, Ray flagged down a shuttle. The little twelve-seater bus was packed with people and luggage. He was happy that the driver announced his airline as the first stop. Pulling over to the curb, the passengers jumped out one at a time. The driver waited patiently as people fumbled with their bags.

Once inside the large airport, he made the grueling walk toward his gate. There were people everywhere, hustling around trying to catch their flights. O'Hare was such a busy airport no matter the day of the week or time of the day.

Passing one of the small restaurants, he vowed to return once he checked in. He always planned to arrive forty-five minutes to an hour before his scheduled departure so that he had enough time to get a bite to eat. The line at the counter was light as he strolled up to the desk.

"Hi, how are you today?" asked the clerk.

"Fine, thanks." He smiled.

"How many are traveling?"

"Just me."

"Okay, do you have your ticket?"

Reaching into his jacket pocket he pulled out the gray folded envelope and handed it to her. She read the information, punched in some data, and returned his ticket.

"All right, Mr. Fuschée, you're all checked in. Seat number 16-C; it's on the aisle. We'll be boarding in about forty minutes. Enjoy your flight."

Gerard lunged out of the cab, throwing two twenties at the driver. "Keep the change," he instructed, running toward the electric doors. Fortunately for him, there was only one person ahead of him at the ticket counter.

"I can help you here, sir," said a cheerful voice further down the line.

"Yes, I was wondering if you had an earlier flight to Philadelphia," he asked, handing the clerk his ticket.

"Let me check. No, sir, the earliest flight we have is the one you're scheduled on."

"What about any other airlines? Can you check to see if they have one?"

"That will take just a second," the man said, punching in the keys on his computer. "As a matter of fact, there's another flight scheduled to depart in about one hour."

"Is it full?"

"Checking. I can put you on standby. Would you like to try?"

"Yes, that would be great. Thank you very much." Gerard got the gate information, grabbed his bags, and headed to the bus. He just had to make that flight, he thought.

Ray ordered a smothered chili dog and a large Pepsi. Anticipating that in-flight dinner service would be light, he decided to eat something that would stick to his ribs. Sitting on one of the stools facing out into the airport, he took in all the different types of people. The thing he enjoyed most about large metropolitan airports was the diversity of folks. O'Hare seemed to represent every class, ethnic group, religious background, and sexual preference he could imagine. The most exciting thing about traveling was that he never knew who he might end up sitting next to on the flight.

Gulping down the rest of his soda, he made his way back toward the gate. Suddenly he felt a vibrating sensation tickling his hip. Moving the jacket away from his side, he glanced down at the small black beeper.

"What now?" he huffed, raising the object to eye level. He read the number on the small screen and then the ensuing message: "Emergency. Please call." *What is going on?* he thought, rushing to a pay phone.

He dialed the numbers displayed in the pager window and waited for the call to go through. It was answered on the first ring. "This is Ray. What's up?"

"Ray, I'm so glad you called. Listen, we have an emergency situation here. I wouldn't have called otherwise," the female dispatcher on the other end said. "Can you come right away?"

"I'm on my way out of town, you know that. In fact, my plane is boarding as we speak. Look, I left firm instructions about the chain of command in my absence. You have ample backup there. I'll call you the minute I get to Philly, okay?"

"Yes sir," the dispatcher replied quietly. Then the line clicked and the dial tone returned.

Ray looked at the receiver for a moment, then slammed the phone back on its cradle. He heard the announcement over the P.A. again, "Final boarding call for Philadelphia." He had to make a quick decision. He knew they could get along without him for one weekend. They could handle it. They'd have to. "Ah, screw it," he said, walking toward the gate. He was entitled to a personal life, wasn't he?

Gerard didn't seem at all concerned about holding up the line. He was determined to get a seat on this flight even if it meant paying someone to give up theirs. He had to make it back to Philadelphia before Georgette went out for the evening. He would marry her tonight.

"Sir, I told you, after we get our reserved passengers boarded, we will start with the standby list," the agent explained in an irritated tone.

"I understand that, ma'am, but I just want to know how far down on the list I am."

"You are fifth. We will call you when we have some more information. I really don't think you have anything to worry about. More than likely we will be able to accommodate you, so please take a seat, sir."

He hated airlines. The agents were abrasive and the flights always overbooked. Now was no exception. He shook his head and then exhaled. There were so many people hanging around the gate. Maybe they were waiting for standby news, or maybe they were waiting to see their loved ones off. He studied their various expressions. Sadness, fatigue, boredom, disappointment. There were a few people who looked vaguely familiar to him. Especially the tall brother over in the corner, grabbing his bags. He wasn't close enough to get a good look at the man's face, but something about the way he moved convinced Gerard he had seen him before. Perhaps the man would sell him his ticket if he explained the situation to him. He would consider asking him if he didn't get called soon.

Ten minutes passed before he finally got his answer. Pulling the small radio mike to her lips, the agent spoke the magical words: "We will now begin taking our standby passengers. Roman, party of two, please approach the counter."

Rising from the gray clothbound seat, Gerard picked up his bags. Patiently standing behind the couple at the counter, he pulled out his ticket when they departed.

"Okay sir, we are still checking our seat availability. We will have a definite answer for you in about five minutes." The agent could tell by his facial expression that he was on edge. "Please sir, be patient. Have a seat until we call you."

Gerard backed away from the counter and leaned up against a pole. He glared at the thin little agent and wondered if she even knew what the odds were of him making this flight.

Twenty-seven

The TV broadcast pierced Georgette's ears as the words "No survivors" kept running through her mind. Sprawled on the floor, she heaved from the lack of oxygen. Fighting to keep her eyes from rolling to the back of her head, she flipped over on her side and assumed the fetal position. She recited a silent prayer. Her lips were clamped shut, her throat achingly dry. She felt like she was dying, like she was giving up the ghost.

The shrill ringing of the telephone broke the spell. Her eyes blurred as she turned toward the steel-gray item resting on the coffee table. Moving her hands stiffly, she clutched the phone. Nervously, she pressed the talk button and cleared her throat, "Hello?" she whispered fearfully.

"Georgette, are you all right?"

"Melinda? Melinda, what's happening? Was that Ray's flight they were talking about?" she asked in a weak voice.

"I'm not sure, sweetheart. That's what I was calling you about."

"Tell me again, Melinda, did they say flight twenty-eight thirty from Chicago?"

"Oh my God, Georgette! I'm so sorry, are you sure he was on that flight?"

"Yes, I'm sure!" she sobbed. "Oh dear God, I can't believe this. Melinda, what am I going to do?" She started crying uncontrollably.

"Georgette, I'm on my way down there. I'm going to send Don over now to check on you. I'll see you in two hours."

Georgette finally mustered up enough strength to reach the sofa. Lying on her back, she let the tears flow freely. Her shirt was heavy with sweat and tears, and she could barely feel her heartbeat.

Cuddling the phone close to her chest, she gasped for air. *Why, Lord? Why Ray?* She immediately flashed back to their weekend in Vail, and everything they had shared since. Staring at the ceiling, she waited for news. She figured that Ray's brother would be calling her soon with the confirmation.

Her thoughts turned to Ray's family. How would his death affect Cheryl and the pregnancy? She was surprised to find that she actually felt sorry for Cheryl. With Ray gone, who was left to come to her defense? Certainly not Gerard or anyone else who knew what she was capable of.

She felt her heart go heavy again. *Gerard.* He was due to come in this evening too. He had spoken of catching an earlier flight. Oh

God, she panicked, what if he was on the plane that crashed as well? Overwhelmed by grief, she leaped off the sofa when she heard the doorbell. Swinging the door open, she cried out gratefully at the sight of the familiar, kind face. She grabbed Don around his neck. She rested her head on his shoulders until she gained enough energy to walk back inside. Suddenly she felt helpless. "Don, I don't know why this is happening to me," she cried. Finally she could let go, there was someone there to watch over her.

Cheryl was at her parents' house when the news flash came across the screen.

"Mom, Dad, come quick!" she yelled as her parents ran into the living room.

"Child, what's wrong with you?" her mother said.

"That flight from Chicago. I think Ray might be on it."

"Oh my sweet Jesus, no! Get me the phone! I've got to call Gloria. Oh Lord, but what if it ain't true? I don't want to worry her. Oh Lord," her mother said, flopping to a chair.

"Cheryl, are you sure?" her dad inquired.

"I'm pretty sure, Daddy. He told me he would be in tonight around seven-thirty. And Ray always, always flew that airline. Oh Mom, I'm scared," she said, covering her face.

"Okay now, let's everybody just calm down until we know for sure. Now, are you supposed to pick him up from the airport?"

"No, his friend is supposed to," she said, wiping her eyes.

"Well, do you know this friend of his?"

"Sort of. I guess I could call and find out for sure if that was his flight," she said, walking over to the phone.

Lifting the receiver from its cradle, she dialed information. "Yes, Philadelphia. I need the number for Georgette Willis." Jotting a number on the pad, she hung the phone back up.

"I'm afraid to call, Mom."

"Then I'll do it, Cheryl. Hand me the phone."

Cheryl picked up the phone and pad and slowly walked toward her mother. But then it occurred to her that she had no reason to fear talking to Georgette. She stopped midway across the room.

"That's all right, I'll call," she said. Besides, she thought, Georgette and she both had Ray in their hearts. She was certain that their mutual love for her cousin would outweigh their differences in a time of crisis such as this.

The ringing of the phone caused Georgette to leap off the sofa.

"Don, would you please answer it? I'm scared," she pleaded in a quivery voice.

As Don reached for the phone, Georgette noticed that his hand was trembling.

"Hello, this is the Willis residence," he said.

"Yes . . . is Georgette there, please?" the tremulous voice on the other end said.

"May I tell her who's calling?"

There was a moment of silence before the reply. "Yes, tell her it's Cheryl."

Stretching the phone toward Georgette, Don told her who it was. She could feel the stream of tears building up in her eyes again as she took the phone from him. Why would Cheryl be calling her unless she had news about the crash? Bracing herself for the worst, she cleared her throat and said, "Cheryl, what is it? Have you got news about Ray?"

"No, Georgette, I'm afraid not. We aren't even sure if that was his flight or not."

The line fell silent again as Georgette searched for the right words.

"Georgette, are you there?"

"Cheryl, I don't know what to say. Ray was booked on that plane. I'm so sorry," she said, the tears falling anew.

Cheryl took a moment to digest the news. There had to be some type of mistake, some mix-up. "Are you sure, Georgette? I mean, do you know if he made the flight for sure?"

"Cheryl, all I can tell you is, it's the same

flight number. If I hear anything, I'll call you right away."

"Please, I would appreciate that very much. If we hear anything over this way, we'll do the same."

Cheryl recited her mother's phone number to Georgette and then hung up. Spinning around slowly to face her parents, she could sense their dismay. She reached out her arms to embrace them, her eyes filling with tears. They knew by her expression that Ray had indeed been on that flight. Cheryl began to cry, and then her eyes widened with pain and she clutched at her abdomen. Her father cradled her in his arms as Cheryl collapsed against him. Mr. Gray looked up at his wife in alarm and yelled, "Honey, we need to get her to the emergency room quick!"

Twenty-eight

Eighty-five minutes had elapsed before Melinda was pounding on Georgette's door. Georgette was resting on the sofa as Don went to the door.

"How did you get here so fast?" Don asked, hugging Melinda as she walked in.

"I broke a couple of speed limits, but I made it safe and sound. Georgette, honey, are you all right?" she questioned, smoothing Georgette's bangs over her forehead.

"I'm hanging in there. Thanks for coming, Melinda."

"Have you found out anything about Ray?"

"Not yet. Cheryl called me awhile back to see if that was Ray's flight. She sounded really shook up."

"Wow, I forgot about her and Ray being cousins and all. Didn't they try to phone their family members in Chicago?"

"I don't think so. I guess she wanted to be sure about the flight number before making any calls. She gave me her mother's number to call if I hear anything and she said she'd

call me if she heard anything. So I guess all
we can do is wait. God, Melinda, I pray to
God he wasn't on that flight."

Georgette lowered her head into the palms
of her hands and wept silently. The sounds
were dry and faint; she was weak from all
the grieving she had done earlier. Melinda
and Don sat patiently on the love seat, waiting for some type of news. Another hour
went by before Georgette reached for the
phone to call Cheryl. It had been several
hours since the crash. Why wasn't there any
news yet? As she lifted the phone to dial
Cheryl's mother's house, she heard a voice
on the other end. She must have picked it
up before it rang.

"Hello, hello? Who's this? Yes, this is Georgette. What? speak up, I can barely hear
you," Georgette instructed. "Who? Hello,
who?" demanded Georgette breathlessly as
she stood up. Don and Melinda moved closer
to her. Melinda watched as Georgette listened to the voice on the phone. She could
see the tears gliding down her friend's face
as Don stood behind her. The yelp from
Georgette's throat caused Melinda to cringe.

"He's dead!" yelled Georgette as she
dropped the phone and collapsed into Don's
arms.

Don laid her down on the sofa while Melinda rushed to her side. "Oh, baby, I'm so
sorry. Who called? Who were you talking to?

Georgette, please answer me. Was that Ray's family?" She was shaking Georgette lightly when Don grabbed her hands.

"Melinda, give her a chance, honey. Georgette," he said calmly. "Was that Ray's family?"

Georgette managed to gather enough strength to pull herself up on the sofa. Looking down at her hands, she studied them a long time. She felt the familiar cheek-burning sensation as her tear ducts opened for what seemed like the hundredth time. She could hear various notes to different songs passing through her mind. Flashes of his face, words he had once spoken. Laughter, the sound of his voice. She glanced up at Don and Melinda as they both circled around her. She smiled faintly at the two of them. They would always be together. How lucky they were. Her mind was racing in a million directions as she looked past them and out the window. Life seemed so fragile suddenly.

"Georgette, sweetie, are you okay? Was that Ray's folks?" Melinda asked again.

Clearing her throat, Georgette clutched Melinda's hands. Her eyes seemed to pierce her friend's very soul.

"No," she said faintly. "It was Gerard's mom."

Cheryl stared at the blue curtains draped around her, trying to see the figures standing behind them. She could hear the voices discussing her condition in hushed tones. She wanted to know what the heck was going on. From what she could gather, her parents were huddled between a man and a woman in white lab coats. Straining to make out what was being said, she edged over to the side of the bed. It was one of those deluxe, relax-when-you-must type of beds. The kind of beds that favor a small plane, a dozen gadgets and controls located off to the sides. Before inclining the bed, with the help of a little white arrow on the side, she called out to her mother.

"Mom, what's going on back there?"

"We will be right there, honey," her mother promised in a soothing voice. The doctor finally snatched the curtain back and stared down at her from over the top of her glasses.

"Ms. Lynn, I'm Doctor Borderson. I would like to keep you overnight, possibly an extra day. It's just a precautionary measure, I assure you. You blacked out and your blood pressure is elevated, and with the pregnancy, that's a big concern. How old are you?"

"Thirty-two, why? Is my baby all right?"

"Everything looks fine, but I want to run a few tests on you and the baby to make sure. Have you ever heard of amniocentesis?"

"Yes, but isn't that usually for women over the age of thirty-five?"

"Well, yes. But given the situation, we think

you should have it done. Look, Ms. Gray, I'm not trying to alarm you. But the test will give us a definitive assessment of the baby's condition. The choice is yours, of course, but either way, I will keep you here overnight, if not two. I'll see you first thing in the morning."

The doctor then disappeared behind a powder-blue wall. What exactly was she trying to say? Better yet, what was it she was trying *not* to say? The concern on her face must have been evident to her mom.

"Cheryl, don't worry, sweetie. Everything is going to be just fine. Let's your father and I have a prayer with you before we leave. You need to get some rest so that my granddaughter will be all right."

"Granddaughter? I think you meant to say grandson, darling," her father teased.

Clasping Cheryl's hands, her father led them in a special prayer. He ended the prayer with, "And Lord, please keep my nephew Ray encamped in your bosom, wherever he might be. Amen."

Still trembling like a fragile branch in the middle of a windstorm, Georgette sipped on some broth. Melinda had done everything a best friend could do to try and alleviate some of the pain. But nothing seemed to help. Georgette was drinking but not tasting, looking but not seeing, listening but not hearing. She was in limbo; her body was there but her mind wasn't.

The phone's jingle made them both jump.

"Just leave it, Melinda, it's probably more bad news."

"Are you sure? What if it's about Ray?" Melinda asked.

"I don't want to know. I can't take anymore." But Georgette must have abruptly changed her mind, because she suddenly reached out and grabbed the phone from Melinda.

"Yes?" she answered in an uncertain tone.

"Georgette? It's me, honey."

"Ray? Ray? Is it really you? Where are you? Oh my God, Ray, I thought you were dead. Where are you? Oh, Ray!" Joy and relief flooded through her.

"I'm sorry that it's taken me so long to phone, baby. I was unable to get away. I was at the airport when my pager went off. The firehouse called about a five-alarm blaze. Baby, it's terrible here. We've lost three children and four adults already. I would have called earlier but it's just mayhem. I only just learned about the plane crash. Georgette, I can't believe it."

"Oh, Ray, thank God you didn't get on that plane. I've been crazy with grief. Cheryl called here wanting to know if I had heard from you yet," she said, sniffling. She could feel the lump bulging in her throat again as she strained to hold back the tears. But it was too late.

"Georgette, baby, I'm sorry. I'm sorry to have worried you so."

She hesitated for a long while before speaking. How could she explain to Ray that her first love, Gerard, was killed in the crash? Furthermore, how would she reveal to Ray the truth about Gerard's marriage proposal? Finally drumming up enough courage to face the inevitable, she whispered to Ray, "Gerard was on that flight."

"What? Gerard? Oh Lord, Georgette, I'm so sorry. Oh my God, has Cheryl heard the news yet?"

"I don't think so. Mrs. Jenkins just called me a few minutes ago. I suppose somebody ought to tell her."

"Listen, I'm going to catch the first thing smoking out of here tomorrow. I'll call you back later with the flight information. Do you think I should wait until I see Cheryl to tell her the news, or give her a call on the phone?"

"You should tell her face to face, Ray. I will call her and let her know you're all right if you like."

"Good. Thank you. I'm afraid if I talk to her I might say something about Gerard. I can't believe this is happening. Are you sure you're going to be all right?"

"I don't know. This is all too sudden, too unexpected. I just spoke to him a few hours ago. He wanted me to meet him—" Her sentence choked off like a weak car battery in below-zero temperature. The lump had risen in her throat again, making it unbearable for her to talk.

"Honey, listen, I'll be there as soon as I can. Just hang on, Georgette. And Georgette, I love you."

Georgette hung up the phone and said a silent prayer. She thanked God for not taking both men's lives. She searched for the piece of paper with Cheryl's mother's phone number on it. His family would be happy to hear that Ray was all right. As she dialed the number, she thought about how Cheryl would react to the news about Gerard. How unfortunate for the child not to ever know his father. A woman answered the phone.

"Yes, ma'am. I'm Ray's friend and I just wanted to let you know that he's all right. He wasn't on that flight after all."

"Oh praise God!" Mrs. Gray yelled. "Did he just call?"

"Yes, just a few seconds ago. He had been summoned at the last minute to fight a large fire and never got the plane. He'll be coming in tomorrow morning."

"Well, I thank God for sparing his life."

"Is Cheryl okay?"

"Actually, dear, she's been admitted to the

hospital. Everything will be fine. They just want to run some tests on her, that's all. She passed out when we were waiting for news about the flight. She's at St. Vincent's Hospital, if you want to call down there."

"Thank you. I might just do that. You have a good evening."

Georgette glanced over to Melinda and Don. They were flipping through some old record albums.

"Melinda, would you drive me down to St. Vincent's Hospital?"

"Sure, Georgette. What's going on?"

"Cheryl's there. As crazy as it sounds, I need to see her."

Melinda didn't say a word. She simply grabbed the keys and starting walking toward the door. What was there to say? It was obvious that a serious task lay ahead of her best buddy. What could she say or do to help her best friend tell her arch rival that the man they once loved and shared was dead?

Upon arriving at the hospital, Georgette told Melinda to wait for her downstairs in the lobby; she didn't want Cheryl to feel like she was being ambushed. After getting the necessary information from the front desk clerk, Georgette walked over toward the two elevators. She suddenly realized how exhausted she was. There were several people waiting for the elevator to reach the lobby level. Georgette stood off to the side, feeling a bit dizzy, while the herd of people entered the elevator. She decided to wait for the next one.

While she waited, her eyes perused the gift shop window, coming to rest on a little pink elephant. How cute, she thought, as she squinted to get a better view of the stuffed animal. For a split second, she thought about running over to the shop and purchasing the item for the patient she was about to visit. But the arrival bell to the elevator had sounded and it was time to board the cabin.

"What floor do you want, miss?" asked a little man in a brown suit, whose face peeked through several large floral arrangements.

"Two please," she said.

Sliding past the other passengers, Georgette stepped out onto the second-floor lobby. It seemed like a circus had paraded through the corridors. The walls were covered in bright pastel washes of yellow, pink, lavender and lime green. The hallway had been decorated with congratulatory balloons, flowers, pictures, and cards, which were plastered all over the place. People were buzzing around with gift baskets; nurses were skipping around with trays; children were playing with books, dolls and various other toys. It really seemed like a major party was taking place.

Searching for room 233, she passed by the nursery and looked in. There were so many little feet, hands, and heads all wrapped in fine cotton. "Wow," she heard herself say. So many babies. She dreamily wondered how pretty her and Ray children would be. A nurse passing by looked at her, smiled, and asked if she could help.

"Could you direct me to room two thirty-three please?" The nurse pointed a little ways down the hall. Georgette exhaled, wiped her forehead, and before long was standing directly in front of Cheryl's room. She knocked twice and waited, until she heard Cheryl's voice inviting her in.

Her face was tired and worn and her expression was blank when she looked up and saw Georgette.

"Did your mom give you the good news about Ray?" Georgette asked.

"Yeah, I just hung up with her. Thank you for calling her."

"Sure. So, is everything all right?"

"I suppose so. I'll know more tomorrow. What brings you here, Georgette? It's not like you to be concerned about my welfare."

Georgette moved closer into the room until she was standing next to a vinyl-covered chair near the bed. "Do you mind if I have a seat?"

Cheryl didn't answer, she just stared at Georgette, trying to figure out the purpose for her enemy's visit. There was a long pause while Georgette settled down into the chair. She took a deep breath.

"Cheryl, I wish I could tell you I *was* here simply to wish you well, but I can't. I needed to come and see you because . . . because . . ." *God,* she thought to herself, *this is going to be so damn difficult!* Cheryl was already down on her luck, down in her looks, and down on her back from all the worrying about Ray.

"Georgette listen, I appreciate your sudden concern, but really, this is not necessary. Now if you don't mind—" Cheryl stopped speaking when she saw the tears forming in Georgette's eyes. Suddenly she realized that something was terribly wrong. "What is it, Georgette? You're scaring me," she said.

"It's Gerard, Cheryl. He was in Chicago for a business trip and was scheduled to come back today. He told me he was going to try and get an earlier flight home." She paused to sniff back the tears before she continued. "It was the flight that crashed. He was on that flight, Cheryl. Gerard was on the plane that went down."

Cheryl's eyes widened in disbelief. Her mouth hung open in shock. She struggled to push herself up on the bed. "You're a liar, Georgette! You're a liar, you lie! Why? Why are you doing this to me? Why? Oh God!" she cried. "You're lying! Get out! Get out!" she screamed. She was crying hysterically and screaming at the top of her lungs.

Two nurses rushed into the room to see what the commotion was. They demanded that Georgette leave and moved to restrain Cheryl. One nurse had to pin her down while the other one sedated her. Georgette hovered by the door until one of the nurses took her arm and led her outside.

"Just exactly what went on in there, miss?" the woman demanded accusingly.

"What? I didn't do anything. I just told her some bad news. She went crazy."

"Well, it's not good for the baby. I'll have to prohibit you from speaking to her again." The nurse returned to Cheryl's room.

Rather than leave, as the nurse expected her to, Georgette sat in the waiting room. She wasn't going to let her relationship with Cheryl end this way. She'd wait until the nurse got off duty and try again.

"Wake up, sleeping beauty."

Georgette opened her eyes. "Ray, what's happening, where am I?" she asked. She had fallen asleep in the waiting room.

"You're in the plush St. Vincent penthouse. Why, don't you remember anything about last night?"

"Sort of," she said, wiping her eyes. "I came down here to tell Cheryl about Gerard. By the way, how's she doing?"

"I'll let her answer that herself. She wants to talk to you."

"Wait Ray!" But it was too late. Cheryl appeared from the shadows. She seemed calm, in control of herself. Almost a different person than she had been a day before. "We should go back to my room. I should stay in bed."

Georgette and Cheryl looked at each other for a long time before Georgette got up and followed Cheryl to her room. Finally Cheryl broke the silence.

Cheryl slid into bed. "Georgette, I just wanted to apologize for my behavior last night. I was hysterical. I appreciate the fact that you came down here to talk to me in person about Gerard. I still can't believe he's gone." She shook her head sadly. "Anyway, that's all I wanted to say. Thanks for coming and I hope everything is okay with you," she concluded and hung her head down.

"Cheryl. How's the baby? Is everything going to be all right?"

Cheryl looked up at Georgette and smiled faintly. "Everything is going to be just fine. You know, Georgette, I feel sort of awkward saying this after all that has happened between us. But you're welcome to visit the baby whenever you like."

Georgette stared at Cheryl, unsure how to answer.

"If Gerard was still living he would have wanted you to know his child. We both know that," she continued.

"Yes, but everything's different now," Georgette said.

Cheryl glanced out the window, then back at Georgette. Taking a deep breath, she said, "I'm sorry about all that stuff, Georgette, I really am."

Georgette stared at Cheryl in bewilderment. She wondered if she would be so sorry if Gerard was still alive. She didn't know whether to comfort the woman with a hug or leave. The fact of the matter was, they no longer had a common denominator, no one left to divide, subtract, or fight over anymore. She could still taste the bitterness of the past as she said, "I guess we're all sorry, now, Cheryl. Where's Ray?"

"He's waiting, hoping and praying that we make some type of peace." Cheryl chuckled. "That boy makes me laugh. I sincerely hope things work out for you and my cousin. I understand he's thinking about transferring to Philadelphia. Perhaps once he gets here, you'll come join us for dinner sometime." She smiled, rubbing her stomach.

"Perhaps." Georgette agreed walking toward the door.

"Well, think about it. Take care, Georgette, and thanks again." The tears were forming in Cheryl's eyes.

"You too, Cheryl, I'm sure I'll see you around." Georgette said, heading out the door.

Ray hugged Georgette and said, "I'm glad to see you guys didn't kill one another."

Georgette was still trying to get a handle on the exchange that she and Cheryl had had. Who would have ever thought that the two of them could be in the same room and act civil toward one another? Ironically, they had Gerard to thank for that. She could feel Ray staring at her.

Finally, she lifted her head up, smiled at him, and said, "So, I hear you're moving to Philly. Does this mean you'll be rooting for the Eagles?"

"Whatever it will take to have you as my wife," he said, grabbing her hands.

"Ray, are you sure you won't mind switching teams?"

"Are you sure you won't mind being Mrs. Fuschée?"

"I'm sure of it." She smiled.

"A Thanksgiving bride? What do you think?"

"Sounds like a plan." She grinned.

"In that case, it's settled. But first, we'll have to get you some rest. Then we can shop for the perfect ring. And after that, we can strategize about how you're going to manage working full-time, washing my clothes, cooking my dinner, cleaning the house and making love to me four times a day," he said, laughing.

Georgette smiled and tickled him. Ray laughed, then pulled her to his chest. Running his hand across the top of her forehead, he brushed her bangs away from her face. He kissed her forehead ever so lightly.

Georgette let out a sigh and whispered, "I love you, Ray."

"I love you, too, my Nubian queen."

SENSUAL AND HEARTWARMING
ARABESQUE ROMANCES FEATURE
AFRICAN-AMERICAN CHARACTERS!

BEGUILED (0046, $4.99)
by Eboni Snoe
After Raquel agrees to impersonate a missing heiress for just one night, a daring abduction makes her the captive of seductive Nate Bowman. Across the exotic Caribbean seas to the perilous wilds of Central America . . . and into the savage heart of desire, Nate and Raquel play a dangerous game. But soon the masquerade will be over. And will they then lose the one thing that matters most . . . their love?

WHISPERS OF LOVE (0055, $4.99)
by Shirley Hailstock
Robyn Richards had to fake her own death, change her identity, and forever forsake her husband Grant, after testifying against a crime syndicate. But, five years later, the daughter born after her disappearance is in need of help only Grant can give. Can Robyn maintain her disguise from the ever present threat of the syndicate—and can she keep herself from falling in love all over again?

HAPPILY EVER AFTER (0064, $4.99)
In a week's time, Lauren Taylor fell madly in love with famed author Cal Samuels and impulsively agreed to be his wife. But when she abruptly left him, it was for reasons she dared not express. Five years later, Cal is back, and the flames of desire are as hot as ever, but, can they start over again and make it work this time?